"Why are you here?" Jenna whispered.

Riley sat down on the side of her bed. "I'm here to protect you, Jenna."

"My name is Faith now," she said in the same quiet voice he remembered, but now with no trace of a Southern accent.

"Sorry. To me, you'll always be Jenna. When was the last time you slept?"

"Not long ago. But every time I close my eyes, I see my attacker."

Riley looked at the slender body under the covers. There had been a time when he wouldn't have hesitated to crawl under those covers with her. He would have gathered her into his arms and promised to protect her from the entire world if he had to.

That time was no longer, now that she had effectively cut him out of her life. He couldn't stop her nightmares; he could only be there to hold her when they did arrive.

Dear Reader,

The kids are on their way back to school, and that means more time for this month's fabulous Intimate Moments novels. Leading the way is Beverly Barton, with *Lone Wolf's Lady*, sporting our WAY OUT WEST flash. This is a steamy story about Luke McClendon's desire to seduce Deanna Atchley and then abandon her, as he believes she abandoned him years ago. But you know what they say about best-laid plans....

You also won't want to miss Merline Lovelace's *If a Man Answers*. A handsome neighbor, a misdialed phone call...an unlikely path to romance, but you'll love going along for the ride. Then check out Linda Randall Wisdom's *A Stranger Is Watching*, before welcoming Elizabeth August to the line. *Girls' Night Out* is also one of our MEN IN BLUE titles, with an irresistible cop as the hero. Our WHOSE CHILD? flash adorns Terese Ramin's wonderful *Mary's Child*. Then finish up the month with Kylie Brant's *Undercover Lover*, about best friends becoming something more.

And when you've finished, mark your calendar for next month, when we'll be offering you six more examples of the most exciting romances around—only in Silhouette Intimate Moments.

Yours,

Leslie J. Wainger
Executive Senior Editor

Please address questions and book requests to:
Silhouette Reader Service
U.S.: 3010 Walden Ave., P.O. Box 1325, Buffalo, NY 14269
Canadian: P.O. Box 609, Fort Erie, Ont. L2A 5X3

A STRANGER IS WATCHING

LINDA
RANDALL
WISDOM

Published by Silhouette Books

America's Publisher of Contemporary Romance

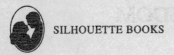

SILHOUETTE BOOKS

ISBN 0-373-07879-X

A STRANGER IS WATCHING

Books by Linda Randall Wisdom

Silhouette Intimate Moments

No More Secrets #640
No More Mister Nice Guy #741
In Memory's Shadow #782
A Stranger Is Watching #879

Previously published under the pseudonym of Linda Wisdom

Silhouette Romance

Dancer in the Shadows #49
Fourteen Karat Beauty #95
Bright Tomorrow #132
Dreams from the Past #166
Snow Queen #241

Silhouette Special Edition

A Man with Doubts #27
Unspoken Past #74
Island Rogue #160
Business as Usual #190
A World of Their Own #220

LINDA RANDALL WISDOM

first sold to Silhouette Books on her wedding anniversary in 1979 and hasn't stopped since! She loves looking for the unusual when she comes up with an idea and only hopes her readers enjoy reading her stories as much as she enjoys writing them.

A native Californian, she is married and has two dogs, five parrots and a tortoise, so life is never boring—or quiet—in the Wisdom household. When she isn't writing, she enjoys going to the movies, reading, making jewelry and fabric painting.

Prologue

Jenna read the instructions on the box for about the tenth time. By now, she knew them by heart, but she still wanted to ensure she understood each and every printed word.

Her hand trembled as she stared at the white stick that, in thirty minutes, would tell her if her life was about to change big-time. Impatiently she hopped from one foot to the other. Jenna was still wearing the hot pink biking shorts and pink and turquoise crop top she'd worn on her run, and her coffee-colored, shoulder-length hair was scooped up into a ponytail.

She should have done it sooner. She could have done the test yesterday or the day before. She could have, but it had taken her four days to get up enough courage to just walk into the drugstore and pick up the kit. And once she'd bought it, she'd stared at the box for more than twenty-four hours, hoping it would divulge its secrets without her doing a thing.

Jenna put the stick down and turned away to set the timer. She refused to obsess about the stick and its secrets. Instead, she took a shower and put on her makeup. She'd just finished dressing when the timer went off. Which meant she had just enough time to have her question answered before she had to leave for the restaurant where she worked as a waitress.

Riley couldn't wait to get home and into the shower to wash off the stink of his job. Not a literal stink, but the miasma of his work. He'd been forced to spend the past week with a man accused of murders that left Riley sick to his stomach. Dealing with such scum was a part of his job as a U.S. Marshal that he didn't like, and today had been worse than usual. Or maybe it was just him.

He couldn't wait to see Jenna. In a few hours she'd be home from work, Riley thought as he walked into their apartment building's large freight elevator. He wasn't sure how he'd gotten so lucky to find someone like her, but he wasn't about to question it. Luck wasn't always on his side, and he had the scars to prove it.

That Jenna, with her bubbly personality and sunshine way of looking at life, was his was something Riley Cooper cherished. And he would, for as long as he had her.

Jenna saw strangers as friends she hadn't met yet, and her artistic talents made her see the world through rainbow-colored glasses.

Riley saw strangers as people to be avoided and the world as black-and-white. Good and bad.

The world he inhabited had no gray areas. The world he inhabited meant he carried a weapon and wore a badge. As a U.S. Marshal, he dealt with convicted prisoners, protected witnesses who were usually on the wrong side of the law to begin with and others no man in his right mind would want to associate with.

His relationships with women had always been short and sweet with no entanglements. Then he'd met Jenna Welles, when an overamorous date had abandoned her by the roadside. He'd been so dazzled by her he'd gone to great lengths to impress upon her that he was reliable, even going so far as to call in a police officer to confirm his trustworthiness.

Of course, the cop had just laughed himself silly and told Jenna that Riley Cooper was nothing but a pack of trouble and she'd be better off without him. But in spite of his words, she still allowed Riley to take her home to her airy loft near Venice Beach. She explained how she'd inherited the loft from a great-aunt who'd been an artist and wanted Jenna to have the same experiences she had. Jenna later explained her relative was a bad artist but had a wonderful head for real estate.

Jenna had proven to be a better artist, even rating a small show the previous year. More than one critic predicted her future would be bright.

It wasn't long after that first night that Riley moved in some of his personal effects, and soon he had more "stuff" in Jenna's loft than at his apartment. After eight months together, they were rarely separated.

Riley entered the apartment and began shedding his clothes, dropping them into the hamper. He stepped into the shower, allowing the hot, steamy water to pour over his upturned face. He had no idea how long he stayed in there, soaping himself over and over. After rinsing off, he reached for a towel and in doing so, happened to glance down at the wastebasket. The words on the white box seemed to jump up at him. Riley's movements were slow as he reached down and picked the box out of the trash.

He knew how badly Jenna wanted children. He also knew she was perfect mother material. Riley had seen her playing with the children on the beach. She just refused to believe he wasn't perfect father material. He didn't need a crystal ball to recognize that knowing there was no hope of children as long as she stayed with him hurt her. Yet she never dropped broad hints. Never talked about babies in front of him and never intimated they'd make the ideal family. A part of him mourned that he wouldn't be the one to give her those children.

He could have been a statue now as he stood there with the box in his hand. There was no mistaking its meaning.

"Jen, can you help us out in the banquet room?" Patti, one of the other waitresses, begged. She quickly filled carafes with coffee. "I don't know why Craig thought Kris and I could handle it by ourselves."

"Sure," Jenna readily agreed. "It's quiet out here anyway. What's going on back there?"

Patti shrugged. "I don't know. One of those businessmen's clubs, I guess. They've been really polite. For once I don't have to worry about pinches."

Jenna picked up a couple of the coffee carafes Patti had already filled.

"Why don't you put those on the head table and I'll take the rear," Patti suggested.

Jenna nodded and headed for the rear of the restaurant. When Craig, the restaurant manager, stopped her, she explained what she was doing and he waved her on.

"Just take them in and leave," he told her. "These guys said they have a lot of business to discuss and don't want to be disturbed after the coffee is served."

"No problem."

She walked down the long hallway toward the banquet room, when the sound of voices coming from the open men's room door momentarily halted her.

"Grieco says all we need to do to pick up the shipment next Thursday is show up at the docks around 3:00 a.m.," a man said in a low voice.

"What about security?" another man asked.

"You know his rules. Grieco prefers dead over alive. You don't leave any witnesses. Just get the shipment and get out. Those computers are worth a lot of money, and we should see our cut within the week."

"That's what I like about him. He knows how to get the job done. I'll take care of it."

Jenna felt a jolt of fear run through her body.

She knew these men meant business. She'd even overheard Riley guardedly talk about Grieco and his operation. Jenna fearfully realized the men were coming back into the hallway. And if she wasn't fast, they'd see her and assume she'd overheard them. She quickly ducked into the ladies' room. Thankful it was empty, she stayed by the door. Remaining still, she held her breath as they walked past. She counted to fifty before she dared crack the bathroom door open and slip out. She hurried to the banquet room door.

Jenna kept her eyes down as she made her way to the head table and set a carafe on each end.

"Hey, sweetheart, can you bring some decaf coffee in here, too?"

The sound of the voices she'd heard from the hallway surprised her so much she almost dropped the empty carafe she'd just picked up. She forced herself to look up at him and offer a faint smile. Jenna knew if she gave any indication she'd overheard their conversation, her life would be worthless. All that mattered was that she go to Riley and tell him what she'd heard.

"Right away, sir," she murmured.

As Jenna walked back toward the kitchen, the conversation she'd overheard echoed inside her head. Grieco ran one of the largest crime operations in the United States. She barely made it to the ladies' room before she was violently ill.

"Honey, what happened to you?" Patti asked, noting her paper white face and trembling hands when she returned to the kitchen.

"I don't know," Jenna whispered.

"With that flu going on, you better go on home.

I'll take care of Craig,'' she assured her before she could protest.

Jenna merely nodded and escaped before she broke down and confessed the story to Patti.

She practically ran home as if she feared that the devil himself was on her heels. Had those men figured out she overheard them and were now following her? What if they followed her to silence her?

Before she entered her apartment building, she checked the rear parking lot and was relieved to see Riley's car parked in its usual spot. By the time she reached the loft, she was almost sobbing.

Seeing Riley seated in the easy chair was enough to release those sobs.

"Oh, Riley," she cried out, running toward him.

She stopped short when she realized there was no smile of welcome on his lips. He held up the white box she'd thrown away earlier.

"I thought you were still on the pill," he said in a cold voice guaranteed to stop her in her tracks.

"I am," she murmured, unable to understand his emotional distance. "But it's not foolproof. I'm more than two weeks late and I thought I should check."

He shot to his feet. "Jenna, you know how I feel about bringing kids into this hell we call a world! I can't do it!"

She stepped back. "Are you saying that you'd want me to destroy our child?" she whispered, feeling a chill steal into her bones.

He shook his head. "No, that's not what I'm saying. I'm saying I can't raise a kid in this world. It wouldn't be right."

Jenna blinked through her tears. "Then it's a good

thing the test came out negative, isn't it?'' She backed up a few more paces. A few minutes ago she had yearned for the protection of his embrace. Now she couldn't bear the idea of his touching her. "You know, I had thought if I was pregnant, you would change your mind. You'd realize how special a child made by us would be.'' She lifted her hand and touched her forehead with her fingertips as if she had a headache. She turned away. At that moment she couldn't even look at him. She thought of what she'd heard in the restaurant. Riley's agitation about the pregnancy kit seemed meaningless now. Jenna started to tell him about it, but her vocal cords felt paralyzed.

She walked over to one of her worktables and picked up a sketch pad along with a pencil. Her movements were jerky as she wrote. When she finished, she silently handed it to Riley.

He looked down, read what she'd written, looked up at her and then down at the paper again.

"You're saying you overheard this?" he asked, tapping the pad with his fingertip.

She nodded. Her movements were still uncoordinated.

"I heard two men talking near the banquet room tonight, and that is what they talked about,'' she said, her voice trembling with fear as she remembered how casual they sounded about murdering people.

"And one of them used the name Grieco? The one man said Grieco was behind this?"

She nodded. Her face was pale, and her eyes seemed to have no life in them.

Riley snagged the phone and punched in a series

of numbers. As he spoke to someone, Jenna headed for the chair he'd vacated. She sat down, curling her legs up under her and leaning into one of the chair arms as if needing the support.

She didn't listen to the words he spoke. They didn't matter to her. As far as she was concerned, she'd done her part. For now, she just wanted to sit there and absorb the pain she felt from Riley's reaction.

True, he'd always said he never wanted children. With what he saw at work, he didn't want to bring a child into a world that had so much evil in it. Jenna, on the other hand, had always thought of herself as someday being a mother, even though she hadn't given herself a timetable. She sensed that when the time was right, it would happen. When she was two weeks late, she'd naturally thought it meant the time was right. And when the test proved to be negative she knew she would just have to wait. She was sad she wasn't carrying Riley's baby. And she felt pity for Riley for his refusal to see just how special the idea was.

Riley's vehement reaction to seeing the box was enough to tell her that she could still plan on having children in the future; she just couldn't plan on him being the father.

She loved Riley so much it sometimes hurt. And she knew he loved her, even if he hadn't actually come out and said the words. It appeared love wasn't enough to make him realize that together they could raise a child who could take on anything the world had to throw at him or her.

"You need to pack a bag," Riley said in a clipped voice as soon as he hung up the phone.

Jenna looked up, dazed by his command. She wanted so badly for Riley to come over and pull her into his arms—to assure her everything would be all right and tell her he would make sure those men were caught and imprisoned.

"Why?"

"Too many people know where you live. We need you to give a statement, then you'll have to go into protective custody." He spoke as if this was a given. As if she had no choice. "There's no guarantee anything will happen, but you might even have to enter the Witness Relocation Program when this is all over."

Jenna shook her head. She looked confused by what he was telling her.

"Why would I have to hide? I'll tell the authorities what I told you. They'll be put in jail, and it will be all over."

Riley wanted to reassure her that everything would be all right. He wanted her to know he would protect her all the way. Except he'd known, from the moment he'd made that phone call, it had been taken out of his hands. There was no way the department would allow him to stay with her, even though he was a U.S. Marshal. Because of their personal involvement, he wouldn't be considered to be any good as a bodyguard. His brain understood the rules, but his body refused to listen.

She was his! He didn't give a damn if the statement was chauvinistic. All he cared about was Jenna. Jenna with the wide navy eyes, and hair, which, when she didn't tie it up, tumbled in loose curls down to her shoulders. Jenna, whose laughter was the song of angels.

Fanciful thoughts weren't a part of his makeup, but the phrase seemed right when he thought of her now.

He should have seen the fear written on her face the moment she'd stepped into the apartment. Instead, like an insensitive bastard, he'd hit her with the accusation about the pregnancy test because he hadn't wanted to believe in that possibility.

The idea of her being pregnant hit him square in the gut and practically drove him to his knees. Riley remembered a case that had haunted his sleep for many months in which an escaped killer had viciously murdered a pregnant woman. He'd never forgotten the husband's anguish. And he'd vowed he would never put himself or Jenna in that situation. There was always the fear that one of the killers he'd arrested in one of his former cases would return for vengeance and take it out on those he loved. He'd seen it happen to others. He wouldn't allow it to happen to him or allow Jenna to become a statistic. So why did he feel so empty when she told him the test was negative?

Now it was up to him to do what he could until someone arrived. If what she said turned out to be true, there would be some happy cops wrapping up more than a few cases. And Grieco's attorneys would be earning their fees in court.

But what about Jenna? What would all of this do to her? She was always so open, so happy. He could only pray what was about to happen wouldn't change what she was now. Could she withstand all the tension and pressure that would be in store for her? He felt she could, but that didn't mean he would allow her to go through it alone.

One thing he did know, he wasn't going to abandon her. If he had to break a few rules, so be it, but he wasn't going to allow her to go on without him.

He walked over and crouched down in front of her. "The men you overheard tonight are killers, Jen," he said softly, taking her hands in his. Finding them cold to the touch, he rubbed them briskly between his own. "Grieco is a killer. He has a good operation going and he won't want anyone screwing it up. Especially a waitress with good hearing. We can't take any chances."

Jenna stared at Riley. She realized the man she was seeing just now wasn't the man who made such glorious love to her or the man who ran with her on the beach at dawn. She didn't see the laughing lover who'd once showered her with gold-foil-covered chocolate coins and told her she was the end of his rainbow.

The man she was looking at was U.S. Marshal Riley Cooper. Stern, cold features that could have belonged to a man, who, more than a century ago, would have tracked down thieves escaping on the backs of horses instead of in cars. This was a man whose world revolved around the law and everything it stood for.

Like it or not, she was now going to enter that world.

She sensed her life would never be the same again.

Chapter 1

Three Years Later in Kansas City

When Faith arrived home after her evening run, she had no idea of the serious consequences that awaited her.

All she cared about was enjoying her favorite time of day. She had enjoyed being outside in the park just before sunset, when the sky was a brilliant collage of pinks, oranges, blues and lavenders and the heat of the day was just starting to dissipate.

After coming home from work, she'd changed into shorts and a tank top and headed out for a well-earned run, as she did every night. She felt that as long as she ran she could forget everything that haunted her nights. She could forget the unwelcome changes that had disrupted her life.

While she ran she told herself to just concentrate on putting one foot down after the other, that all she had to do was run long enough to become so tired she could sleep that night without dreaming.

Faith always ran the course mapped out for dedicated joggers. She never bothered to look at any of the other runners who were on the track at the same time. All she cared about was tiring herself out. By the time she finished her six miles, she would be aching and ready to return home and fix herself some dinner.

Tonight, she'd stopped at the grocery store for a bottle of water and had taken her time walking home as part of her cooldown. By the time she unlocked her front door, she was ready to prepare her dinner. She stepped inside her house and had barely closed the door behind her when she felt an arm grab her around the neck, pulling her tightly against a rock-hard body. A powerful hand had covered her mouth so swiftly she'd no chance to take a breath much less scream.

"Hey, there, Jenna." The smell of beer had her gagging with revulsion as thick lips caressed her skin. "Guess you thought you were pretty smart, huh? That they had you well hidden away. Guess what? We're smarter."

She couldn't stop the hot tears that dripped onto the back of her attacker's hand. It had been some time since she'd felt this kind of fear racing through her veins.

But this time was much worse. This time she knew no one would come in at the right time to save her. She knew that tonight she faced her death.

* * *

Two days later on the Kauai Coastline

"Talk about retiring in style, ole buddy. Who do you have to kill to get digs like this?"

Riley walked out of the surf with a surfboard under one arm. Rusty brown hair hung down in wet, dripping tangles to his deeply tanned shoulders. His mouth twisted with a wry smile as he faced his one-time partner who stood at the edge of the beach.

"What are you doing here, Gaines?" He stuck the end of the surfboard into the sand.

Dave Gaines grimaced as grains of sand found their way into his highly polished black leather loafers as he crossed the wide expanse of beach.

"I thought I'd fly over and see how the other half lives." He waved his hand to encompass the sprawling house behind him. "Not too shabby a beach shack, partner. I would have rung the doorbell, but hell, you don't have one. For all I know you probably don't even have electricity. I already know you don't have a phone."

"Since I don't want company, I didn't see any use in having one." Riley pushed his hair away from his face. "Pretty formally dressed for a casual visit," he nodded to indicate his ex-partner's suit that was rapidly wilting under the Pacific sun. "Why don't you cut the bull and tell me why you're here," he said, indicating the manila envelope Dave held in one hand. "Neither one of us was much for small talk."

Dave shook his head. "Can't blame a guy for trying. We need your help, Riley. One of your witnesses received a very unwelcome visitor a few days ago."

Riley laughed. "What do you want, sympathy?

I'm out of that, remember? Benedict accepted my
letter of resignation. It's great being retired. I have a
nice monthly pension, and I can surf anytime I want
to. You're a smart guy, Dave. I have faith in you to
take care of any problems that crop up. Hell, just tell
Benedict to use whoever took my place. I'm too
happy being a surf bum.''

Dave looked at his friend's barely there swim
briefs with something akin to envy.

"Hey, I hear you, buddy, but this one's important.'' His grin dimmed. ''Grieco's thugs tracked
down Jenna.''

Riley froze at the name that invaded his dreams
whenever the nights became too long and lonely.
Nights when a bottle of scotch wouldn't do the trick.

He swallowed hard as he thought of Grieco's men
and what they could do to a person.

"They tracked her down? Is she—'' He couldn't
voice the words.

Dave shook his head. "She was lucky, but only
because a neighbor heard her screams and called the
cops.'' He opened the manila envelope and pulled
out several photographs, which he held out to Riley.

Riley hesitated before taking them out of Dave's
hands. The color photographs were a graphic testa-
ment of what violence could do to a woman.

He could see the pain in her shimmering navy blue
eyes. Dark bruises dotted her cheekbones and one
eye was swollen. Blood had crusted over on a split
lip, and a nasty cut bisected one brow and another
marred her chin. Her coffee-colored hair lay in tangled clumps around shoulders marred with more
bruises. The other photos showed further bruising

and cuts on her body. She stood there looking like a lost child who had just visited hell. He saw only bare traces of the Jenna he remembered. She hadn't changed her hair color or length during the past three years. But she didn't look the same to the man who knew her so well.

He swore darkly as he studied each photo that showed a woman physically and emotionally devastated.

"Was she raped?" he asked in a raw voice as he returned to the first photo. He didn't want to think of any further indignities that could have been done to her. He knew only too well how harsh a man could be to a defenseless woman. If she'd been touched that way, he swore he would kill the man...slowly.

Dave shook his head. "I don't think rape was his game. The suspect tore her clothing and played some nasty head games with her. He wanted her terrified of him the entire time. He did such a good job she's still terrified. He escaped and now she's afraid he'll come back to finish the job."

Riley couldn't take his eyes off the wounded face and eyes that showed the terror Dave was talking about. He could feel raw anger burning in his gut.

"What about her hands?" he asked in a low voice.

"Her hands?"

"Her hands! Dammit, did he hurt her hands!"

Dave was taken aback by the violence brewing within Riley. He should have been used to it. He and Riley had worked together for twelve years before Riley got out. He knew just what Riley and Jenna had been to each other before their world blew up in their faces. He knew why they were apart and how much their separation had initially affected Riley. He should have realized that just because three years had passed it didn't mean Riley was over her.

"He broke her right forefinger and middle finger." He sounded reluctant, as though he anticipated how Riley would take the news.

Riley sorted through the photos again as the other man kept on talking.

"The cops called an ambulance once they saw her. One of them found our card in her purse and called our office from the hospital. Someone went down to talk to her, but she refused to tell him anything. She said she wanted you. When she was told you were no longer with the Marshal's Service, she got pretty hysterical. They called me in, and I flew out there immediately. She didn't want to see me, either." Dave took a deep breath. "The doctor finally had to give her a sedative. We need you, buddy. We need you bad. Even more important, Jenna needs you."

I always thought U.S. Marshals rode in on big horses and cleaned up the rowdy cow towns. I'd like to paint you that way one day, Riley.

Riley closed his eyes, but it didn't stop the voice he could hear deep inside his brain. A voice that was soft and musical, with the faintest hint of a Southern accent. He used to listen to her and think of rolling green lawns and gentlewomen walking in their pastel-colored crinolines and carrying parasols to protect their magnolia skin from the sun.

Except she hadn't wanted him when life had taken a turn for the worst. Although he'd wanted to be there for her, she had rejected him.

"I'm out of it, Dave," he said finally. "If she

needs someone, get Marcia. They got pretty close while we were...while we knew each other,'' he spoke haltingly.

He wondered if Jenna would have become involved with him if she'd known she would lose her ability to create art that was so good the world was meant to see it. By all rights he should have driven her home that first night and not sought her again. But then he would have lost out on something that was so perfect that the light had gone out of his world the night she'd overheard Grieco's men and he'd known a change was inevitable.

In the end, she'd had no choice but to go into the Witness Relocation Program, which meant she had to leave all facets of her former life behind. Except Riley hadn't meant for her to leave him behind. From the moment he knew she would be entering the Program, he started making arrangements to do the same. Superiors were unhappy with his decision, but he didn't care. He just knew Jenna wasn't going alone. What he hadn't planned on was her not wanting him with her.

He felt the pain every day after a marshal escorted her out of state. Within a short amount of time she had a new identity and was settled into a new life. Riley had no idea where she was. He'd been barred from learning, and the frustration of not knowing only made matters worse for him. Jenna might have been out of sight, but she was never out of mind. His work wasn't enough for him no matter how hard he threw himself into it. In the end he'd handed in his resignation and left with the intention of turning into a true beach bum. He'd done a pretty good job of it, too.

Dave looked stunned by his announcement. "You can't do that to her. She's alone, Riley, and she's asking for you."

"You, of all people, know I can't go back."

"They found her without you, Riley. Which means someone with a very good sniper scope could still show up. You can't put her in any more danger than she already is by going up there."

All Dave got for his speech was stony silence. Riley started to turn away. Dave grabbed his shoulder and pulled him around.

"Damn you, Riley! Do you know what I found when I flew out there? I found a woman who was so scared she couldn't stop crying. And then she kept apologizing for crying. That bastard terrorized the hell out of her. He left her feeling so afraid she can't sleep unless the lights are on. She refused to be examined until I was called. And then I had to promise I'd be there as soon as I could. She just about lost it in there."

Riley's jaw was clenched tightly to keep him from roaring with anger. Jenna looked delicate, but he'd always felt she was like the willow tree and could bend in the face of adversity. He'd always thought she was safe. She had a new life, maybe even a new love. Maybe even a family. She sure didn't want him in her life, so why would she ask for him now?

"Why don't you call her boyfriend?"

Dave shook his head. He didn't bother to mask his disgust. "Come on, Riley. Did you honestly think she would want a man in her life? She loved you, man.''

Riley didn't want to think about it. "How is the case being handled?"

"The local cops are putting it down to her surprising a burglar. Instead of knocking her out and taking what he could, he settled for playing some pretty nasty games with her. There were no fingerprints, and he wore a ski mask, so she couldn't see his face.''

Riley took a deep breath and looked off to the pounding surf behind him. The waves had been perfect that afternoon. He had been able to go out there on his board and ride them with no other intention than to see how long it would take for him to spill. This was the life he had made for himself. He told himself he wanted nothing more than the surf and an occasional evening with a willing woman. The first was easy. The second wasn't. Not when he saw Jenna's face everywhere he went.

"Where is she now?" he asked finally.

"Kansas City."

I've always hated the cold. I like to live where there's water and lots of sun.

"Couldn't get her much farther from the beach, could you?" Riley muttered. "Oh, hell." He crushed the photographs in his hand. He stared at his friend and held out his arm, pointing at him as he made his demands. "I'm an outside consultant. I do it all my way, and I don't come cheap."

"You know I can't promise anything like that!" Dave argued.

"Benedict will go along with it and you know it.

That's the only way I come on board. I have to be in complete charge. If I take her, only I will know where she is. The only person I will contact is you. If I set her up in a new life, only I will know about it. And I'm going to change her appearance, which should have been done three years ago. Somebody sure screwed up. This way we know it won't happen again.''

Dave exhaled the deep breath he had been holding. "All right, but Benedict won't be happy."

"Ask me if I care." Riley hefted his surfboard back under his arm and started up to the house. "Have a beer while I shower and change?"

Dave settled for slipping off his loafers and socks before following.

"No wonder life has been so quiet," he shouted at Riley's back. "I didn't have to work with a son of a bitch like you."

"Yeah, well, that SOB is back," he said wryly.

Twelve hours later Riley stared at the nondescript house in the quiet neighborhood.

"We told her she couldn't go back to her apartment," Dave explained as the two men climbed out of the car. "I handpicked the men who are with her now."

Riley thought of the automatic nestled against his spine, artfully hidden by the pine green polo shirt that hung over his jeans. He might be back in action, but he refused to wear a suit or cut his hair. It hung loose around his shoulders.

At the door Dave identified himself to the marshal, and the two men stepped inside. Riley stared grimly at the man seated on a couch. An open pizza box sat on the coffee table and a baseball game played on the television.

"You feed the lady any of that pizza?" His gaze lingered on the box that was almost empty.

One of the men, who had been introduced to Riley as Jim Case, shifted uneasily under the hard look Riley now directed his way.

"She hasn't eaten all that much," he muttered. "She says she's not hungry, and we haven't wanted to push anything on her. She's still feeling pretty raw from the attack."

Riley looked around at the furnishings that were the usual issue for any safe house. He didn't see any sign of a third agent.

"Where's the female marshal?" he rapped out. "There's supposed to be one here for her."

"She'll show up in an hour or so," Stan, the other marshal, replied. "Ms. Carson stays to herself in the master bedroom." He grinned. "Easy duty for us. She's easy to look at, and she's quiet. Wish my wife was like that."

"What the hell do you guys think you're doing?" Riley exploded. "Do you realize just who you're looking after? Before she was put into the Program, this lady was well on her way to becoming one of the leading artists of our time. If she hadn't been at the wrong place at the wrong time, she would have been world famous by now." He bore down on the man.

"Hey, buddy." Dave laid a restraining hand on his arm. "Their idea of art is something their kids do in kindergarten."

Riley stepped back, but the fear on the other man's face said he knew if it hadn't been for Dave, he would have been picking himself up off the floor.

Riley shook off Dave's restraining hand, threw a look filled with disgust at the other men and headed for the rear of the house. It wasn't hard to guess that the only room with a closed door was the one housing Jenna Welles.

"Her name's Faith Carson now," Dave called after him.

Riley's hand lingered on the doorknob, but he found he couldn't turn it. He lifted his other hand and softly rapped his knuckles against the door.

"Miss Carson, may I come in?" He wasn't surprised there was no answer. He turned the knob and pushed the door inward.

The woman lay curled up on the bed with her back to him. The drapes were drawn so all she had to look at was a dark blue and green floral print. She didn't turn, although she had to have heard the door opening.

"Hey there, Smitty."

Her head snapped up and around when she heard the husky voice she hadn't heard for years. Jenna had forgotten the nickname Riley had bestowed on her once when they'd stopped at a little out-of-the-way bed-and-breakfast and she had laughingly checked them in as Mr. and Mrs. Smith.

She had forced herself to forget who she'd been. As it was, she lived with a constant reminder of the life she'd once lived and would never be able to return to. The familiar voice brought tears to her eyes as she stared at the man she'd been so deeply in love with, who had abandoned her when she'd needed him most.

"Why are you here?" she whispered, not moving from her fetal position.

Riley closed the door behind him as he stepped into the room. He walked around the bed and sat down on the edge, his hip bumping against her knees. He took her hands in his and found them ice-cold. The splints on her fingers were a reminder of her trauma, along with the deepening bruises on her face. She was dressed in badly wrinkled shorts and a T-shirt that showed spots of dried blood. There was no doubt she had come home from the hospital in these clothes.

He felt the anger boiling up inside him until he thought he might erupt. Those bastards! Why hadn't they taken those clothes away from her and given her fresh clothing? Hadn't they checked her to see if she was in pain?

"You told the cops you surprised a burglar, didn't you?" he said quietly, touching her hands lightly. It was as if the past few years hadn't happened and he'd only been gone a few moments.

She shrugged. "It was easier to make them believe that than tell them the truth. I knew your office wouldn't want them to know the truth." Her words were slightly garbled because of her lower lip. He hazarded a guess that she probably had some cuts inside her mouth, too. "Why are you here? Dave said you didn't work for them anymore."

"I couldn't let one of my cases fall into someone else's hands, could I?" he said lightly. But there was no answering smile. Only a shadowy pain in her eyes. He thought of a fragile doll with a backbone of steel. Except he didn't see any of that steel in her now.

She slowly drew her hands back and placed them gingerly on the bedspread.

"It was nice of you to visit." She spoke in the same quiet voice he remembered, but now it had no hint of a Southern accent.

"This isn't a visit, Jenna. I'm here to protect you."

"My name is Faith now."

He shook his head. "Sorry, to me you'll always be Jenna, no matter what name they gave you."

Jenna Welles, now Faith Carson, studied Riley. His face was a deep bronze. His hair hung to his shoulders, and there was a harshness in his voice she didn't remember from before. There wasn't anything familiar in his style of clothing. At first she felt as if she was looking at a total stranger.

Then she stared into his jungle cat eyes. A deep brown with glittering flakes of gold that almost seemed to glow in the dark. The eyes she remembered. They always glowed a deep gold when he made love to her. She noted the lines carved in his rough-hewn face that hadn't been there before. She could sense the anger simmering deep within him. Yet he had always been unbearably gentle with her.

She had thought of Riley all the time the faceless man had terrorized her with his soft-spoken promises of pain just before he carried them out. She'd hugged memories of his strength as pain seemed to radiate all through her body with each blow directed at her, each light slice of the knife across her skin bringing on even more agony. At first she had prided herself on not begging him to stop, in not screaming. Then the pain took over, and her screams were ceaseless. She was still screaming, unaware her attacker had escaped, when the police arrived and tried to help her.

While she lay in the hospital's Emergency Room, she'd clung to the hope that Riley would arrive and make things better. She kept asking the other marshals to contact Riley. She needed him. Except it was Dave Gaines who had arrived. That was when she shut down. She mentally and emotionally had withdrawn from the world around her, because it was the only way she felt safe. She'd allowed the marshals to take her from the hospital to this house. She hadn't even bothered to ask to return to her house for her things. By then she just didn't care what happened to her.

"When was the last time you slept?" Riley asked her.

She hadn't expected that question. She'd expected him to immediately ask her about the man who had attacked her, what he'd said and anything else she might remember. The others had asked all those questions and more, but she wasn't able to help them very much.

She lifted one shoulder in a shrug. "Not long ago." She knew she looked like hell. She didn't want to tell him that she didn't want to sleep. Every time she closed her eyes she saw her attacker. Unthinkingly, she shuddered.

Riley stood up. With ease, he gathered her up in his arms and reached down to pull back the covers.

He carefully laid her back down and placed the covers over her. She didn't take her eyes off him as he walked over to the adjoining bathroom. He opened the door a few inches and flipped on the light. He walked back to the bed and sat down on the other side with his back braced against the headboard.

"Sleep, Smitty." His voice flowed over her like warm water.

She didn't consider doing anything else. She obediently closed her eyes, and with the knowledge Riley was watching over her, she fell into the first deep sleep she had had in days.

Chapter 2

Jenna's sleep brought terror. If she slept, she dreamed. And when she dreamed, her attacker returned to haunt her. He whispered vile things in her ear, he smiled as he caused pain in every part of her body. And his eyes. Pale blue shot with silver, they were cold as ice as they watched her writhe in agony under his professionally placed blows meant to cause excruciating pain. She whimpered and tried to move away from his tight grip. When he didn't relent, she lashed out with her fists. She didn't know why she tried to fight back since he only hurt her more. She wanted to scream, but her lips couldn't make any sound. She could feel the cries rising in her throat, but they couldn't go any farther.

"Jenna. Jenna." Someone was shaking her. Not hard enough to hurt. Just firmly enough to bring her away from her sleep-filled terror. "You're dreaming. Open your eyes, Smitty."

"Please, don't hurt me!" she gasped at the same time her eyes popped open. An evil man wearing a ski mask wasn't laughing at her. She stared at Riley, whose eyes were dark with concern. A narrow stream of light shone across his face. Her raspy breath sounded loud in the silence as she gulped in much-needed air.

She flinched when Riley reached up to brush her hair from her face. She didn't miss his pained expression at her recoil.

He got off the bed and went into the bathroom. Jenna pulled her legs up until she could rest her chin on her drawn-up knees. She kept her eyes on the light shining from the bathroom. Light meant safety.

A moment later, he came out carrying a damp washcloth. He sat on the bed and began wiping her face. The cool cloth felt good against her hot skin.

"He came back," she whispered.

"He will for a while."

Jenna was grateful he didn't try to assure her it was only a dream. She didn't want to hear him tell her she was safe now, if it was a lie. One thing she could count on was Riley never lying to her. If anyone did the lying in their relationship it had been her. She'd lied when she left him; she *had* still loved him.

"You know you'll have to move out of the state."

She nodded. "They already told me that. It doesn't matter. I don't have anything to keep me here, anyway." She tugged the covers up over her shoulders as she lay down with her back to him.

Riley looked at the slender body under the covers. There had been a time when he wouldn't have hesitated in crawling under those covers with her. He would have gathered her into his arms and promised her that nothing bad would happen anymore. He would protect her from the entire world if he had to.

That time was no longer, since she had effectively cut him out of her life. He got off the bed and settled back in his chair. He couldn't stop her nightmares from haunting her, but he could be there to hold her when they did arrive.

Jenna felt groggy when she woke up. The light coming through the blinds told her it was late morning. Her senses told her she was alone in the room. She sat up in bed and rubbed the remaining sleep from her eyes.

Even after taking a shower and dressing, she still felt out of sorts. The rumble of men's voices compelled her to move toward the door where she opened it a scant inch.

"You can't talk to me that way, Cooper."

"I don't give a damn if I hurt your feelings, Chalmers." Riley's voice was low pitched and throbbing with fury. "You mishandled this case from the beginning. Then you bring in two insensitive idiots who don't seem to notice if their charge has eaten or not. They don't even bother to find out if she needs anything. Even a speck of comfort. And where's the female agent?"

"Women agents have always been here for her."

"Really? Where? They're sure not here now."

Jenna winced at the cutting sound of Riley's voice. Obviously the other man didn't understand that Riley didn't suffer fools lightly nor accept excuses. She opened the door a little wider.

The other man was wearing a dark suit and had the look of a man aware of his power. Riley was still wearing the wrinkled chinos and cotton shirt he'd arrived in. There was no doubt at that moment Riley was the one in charge.

"Excuse me, gentlemen, but is there a chance of getting some breakfast?" she asked in a soft voice.

Riley spun around first. The other man stepped forward with his hand outstretched.

"Miss Carson, I'm U.S. Marshal Chalmers. I've been assigned to your case."

She smothered a smile as she shook his hand. She wondered what he'd think if she told him she felt as if she was shaking the hand of a dead fish. The faint twist of Riley's lips told her he'd already echoed her thoughts.

"I thought Marshal Cooper would be taking care of me," she said softly.

Chalmers sent Riley a quelling look before turning back to Jenna.

"*Mister* Cooper is no longer a part of this situation. It appears he wanted to make sure you were safe. But by showing up, he has only further endangered your life. One of my men will be assisting you in your new relocation, and we will have your new life set up within forty-eight hours. Since you've been through this before, I'm sure you won't have any problem adjusting."

Jenna decided she didn't like the smooth-talking man. It was apparent he spent his time behind a desk and not on the streets. She glanced at Riley to see his reaction to this announcement. The dark flare in his eyes and the stiff set of his jaw told her he wasn't happy with what he was hearing. She latched on to that thought like a drowning woman.

"I can't trust your men any longer, Marshal Chalmers," she said softly. "I won't go with anyone but Riley."

Chalmers's smile froze. "If you wish to remain safe in the Witness Relocation Program you have no choice but to do whatever we deem necessary to keep you alive. Riley has too many enemies who could easily recognize him, now that he's out of hiding, and attack you both."

Her eyes didn't leave his. "Riley will keep me alive. I trust him. I don't know you." That she didn't trust him was unspoken but the words were still there.

The slick smile turned ugly for a second before he remembered himself. "Miss Carson, I can't guarantee your safety if you go with Cooper."

"Doesn't seem you've been doing too much so far," Riley said lazily. "Don't worry, Chalmers. You're off the hook. I already got authorization to take Miss Carson out of here while your men do their job in tracking down Grieco." He stuck his hands in his pockets and rocked back and forth on his heels. "Unless you need some help with that, too."

Dave, who had been standing in the background, muttered something under his breath. He walked over and took her arm.

"How about eggs, bacon and French toast?"

Her eyes widened at the idea of so much food.

"That way the adults can discuss your fate without

you having to hear all the bad words," he said in a low voice as he escorted her toward the kitchen.

Riley's gaze spit bullets as he turned back to Chalmers.

"Are you always this stupid, or is this just for my benefit?"

"Look here, you son of a—"

The expression on Riley's face stopped the man cold.

"Miss Carson is under the U.S. Marshal's protection, and so far I haven't seen that kind of protection," Riley said in a low, deadly voice. "The lady has been found out, almost beaten to death and needs some reassurance she'll be alive to see tomorrow. I haven't seen any of that coming from you. I'm going to make some arrangements, and then she and I are out of here."

Chalmers stared at him for a moment before he stalked out of the house.

"Friendly sort," Riley muttered, turning around and following his nose. The aroma of coffee and bacon was more than enough to entice him.

He walked into the kitchen and saw Jenna sitting at the kitchen table with a plate filled with French toast in front of her. Another plate covered with scrambled eggs and rashers of bacon was nearby.

"I can't possibly eat all of this," she told Dave as he set a pot of coffee on a hot pad.

"I have an idea you'll have some help." He sent a glance in Riley's direction.

Both sets of eyes watched Riley cross the kitchen to the telephone. He snagged himself a coffee cup and filled it as he punched in a number.

"Hey there, darlin'," he murmured. "Yeah, it's me. Think you can help me out today?" His chuckle was pure sin. "You wish. Naw, I need a complete makeover for someone, and I know if anyone can perform miracles, it's you. I'll make it worth your while." He waited as he sipped his coffee. "An hour? Good. I'll send someone to pick you up. Bring everything you might need for an overhaul. Great. Thanks." He hung up and leaned against the counter as he finished his coffee. "Glad to see you kept your culinary skills, Gaines."

He walked over, grabbed a chair and spun it around so he could rest his arms on the chair back. He stared at Jenna for several moments.

"If you think I'm going to share my breakfast you have another think coming." She defiantly picked up a piece of bacon and bit down on it with a satisfying crunch.

Riley winced. "Someone's coming over in an hour to help turn you into someone else." He glanced up at Dave. "Think you can pick up Sassy for me?"

"Sassy?" Jenna repeated the name. "This should prove interesting." She turned to Riley. "Do you mind? I haven't eaten all that much in the past few days and I'd like to enjoy this meal. From the way you're talking about taking over my life, I may not get the chance to eat a decent meal for some time."

Riley held up his hands in a gesture of surrender and backed off. Secretly he was glad to see she was willing to bite him back. It would be easier to keep her going if she was angry. He had started planning their trip from the moment he'd gotten up, and it wasn't going to be easy.

"Then I suggest you eat as much as possible." He refilled his coffee cup on the way out.

Jenna's appetite suddenly deserted her.

"Knowing Riley, it might be a good idea to eat hearty," Dave suggested.

She shrugged. "It isn't easy when my stomach is still doing flip-flops."

Dave didn't need explanations. "He felt pretty raw when you left."

Jenna kept her gaze on the table. It was safer there. "I couldn't allow him to give up his career to enter the Program with me," she murmured, tracing a random pattern on the plate with her fork. "He was meant for big things."

"Riley was always his own man. He never wanted the glory or perks that went with it. Probably because he knew you can't climb the ladder when you're ticking off everyone hanging on the rungs above you."

Jenna smiled. "Riley does tend to speak his mind whether you want to hear it or not." She speared a cube of French toast and dipped it in syrup. She chewed and swallowed. "I prefer to evade the issue, and he would just dive right in. I'd forgotten that trait of his." Her voice trembled.

Dave patted her shoulder. "You'll be fine, Jenna." He left her alone with her thoughts.

"No, I won't. I was fine before, when I convinced myself I was over Riley."

"Well look at you! Are we goin' macho or what?" Scarlet-polished talons threaded through Riley's hair. "I love all this hair, darlin', but you could use some shapin'."

Riley grinned at the woman standing before him. "Sweetheart, the last person I want near me with a pair of scissors is you. Besides, I have someone else in need of your expertise." He left the room and came back with Jenna in tow. "Sassy, this is Jenna. Jenna, this is the woman who's going to turn you into a new person."

Jenna gazed wide-eyed at the woman standing before her. Even without the leopard-print stiletto backless heels she had to be over six feet tall. Her strapless, leopard-print catsuit showed off a body that didn't have an ounce of fat on it. Jenna's gaze didn't seem to move from the black enamel panther pendant hanging from a thick gold chain. Matching earrings swung to and fro.

"Sassy used to work in Hollywood fixing up the rich and infamous," Riley explained.

"Until I decided to head for home and open my own place here," Sassy said in a throaty voice. "What do you want me to do, Riley?"

"Whatever it takes to make her look like someone else. I don't want *anyone* to recognize her."

Sassy tipped her head from one side to the other as she surveyed Jenna in a businesslike manner.

"Honey, when I get through with her, her own mother won't even recognize her. Why don't you use those lovely muscles of yours to bring in my equipment? Now, Jenna, sweetie, why don't you lead me to the bathroom. We've got some work ahead of us."

Jenna felt swept away as Sassy took charge. The hairdresser didn't waste any time as she washed her hair and slathered it with a conditioner.

"Honey, your hair is crying out for a moisture

pack," she chattered, folding a towel around the peppermint scented strands. "Your skin can use some help, too. Good thing I brought a little of everything." She placed her hands on her hips and studied Jenna. "Are you willing to go along with anything I do?"

"Do I have a choice?"

"We can always compromise. I'm talking about cutting and coloring."

Jenna gulped. The most she'd done to her hair for the past few years was a trim every six months.

"Riley said you were to do whatever was necessary."

Sassy's laughter was bold and bawdy. "Then let's give the man a big surprise. He's an impatient stud, but that's all right. There's nothing more excitin' than an impatient stud." She rummaged through the large tote bag that carried the tools of her trade.

Jenna stared at the array of tools Sassy laid out on the counter.

She had a strong feeling her life was going to take a radical turn.

"How long does it take to do somebody's hair?" Riley grumbled as he checked his watch for the fifth time in the past hour.

"You told Sassy to give her the works," Dave said as he idly flipped through a magazine.

"I meant give her a haircut so she doesn't look the same."

Dave looked past Riley. "I'd say she definitely looks different."

Riley spun around. Jenna, or at least the woman he thought was Jenna, stood in the doorway.

Her hair was several inches shorter in a layered cut and was now a glittering mass of bronze and golden blond strands that lay against her nape and cheeks. Her eyebrows were darker and seemed to have more of an arch while her eyes were shadowed and looked luminescent. A bronzing gel had been smoothed onto her skin to give it a darker glow.

"She looks like she's barely out of high school!"

Sassy didn't bat an eye under Riley's explosion.

"Honey, you wanted a completely different look and you got it." She smiled, clearly proud of her work. "I told her I'd send over some clothes more fitting to her new image."

Riley sat down hard on a chair.

"I never thought it would be so fascinating to look younger," Jenna commented wryly.

Riley's reply was more profane.

Dave grinned. "What are you going to do with Riley, Sassy?"

The hairdresser sashayed over to Riley. "Anything he wants, sugar." She shot Riley a come-hither smile. "Come with me, darlin'. I'm going to turn you into a new man." She glanced at Dave over her shoulder. "And you go on over to my shop and take Renee shopping. I'll call and give her sizes."

"I could do this at home, you know," he muttered, pushing himself out of his chair.

"See what a little shaping will do?" Sassy declared, after she brushed Riley's hair back and tied it with a leather thong. "Very sexy, honey." A mirror was thrust into Riley's hand.

Riley barely glanced at his reflection before he set the mirror down. "So tell me, *Myron,*" he said as he stressed the name, "why did you turn a mature woman into a teenager?"

Sassy winced at the mention of his real name.

"She had the face for it as long as the hair, makeup and clothing fit the image. You wear some sexier clothes, look the image of a wealthy man with nothing more important than escorting his niece to wherever you're going, and no one will give the two of you a second glance."

Riley would have liked to argue with the hairdresser on the observation, but he couldn't. Sassy had helped him out several times with disguises. Her years working in the film industry had helped hone her skills, and it had been a stroke of good fortune that she'd settled in Kansas City.

"I saw the way you looked at her, darlin' and that wasn't some uncle looking at his beloved niece," Sassy told him. "Something tells me she was the one you had your briefs in a twist about."

The dark glare in Riley's eyes had felled many a man. Sassy didn't back down an inch.

"Aw, honey, you know better than to try staring me down." Within moments everything was packed in her tote bag.

"I'm back," they heard Dave call out from the back of the house.

Sassy and Riley met Dave in the living room as he set down a variety of bags.

"You really think we have an unlimited budget, don't you?" Riley asked Sassy.

"No, I just knew you wouldn't let one of your people leave without the right accessories. Bye, Jenna, you hold on tight, you hear. This man will keep you safe." Sassy took Riley's arm. "You can drop me off, can't you?"

Riley didn't look at Jenna as he left. After he dropped Sassy off at her shop, he headed for Jenna's apartment. Breaking in was no problem.

The interior was dark, so he waited a moment to allow his eyes to adjust to the dim light.

Overturned furniture told him of a struggle. He crouched down and touched dark brown spots marring the beige-colored carpeting. He didn't need the lights on to verify it was dried blood. Fury boiled deep down as he visualized a man beating Jenna.

Another visualization entered his mind. A more welcome one. He couldn't see the face of the man he was beating to a pulp, but it didn't matter. He was too happy giving him what he deserved.

He straightened up and went into the bedroom. That room was also a mess, but not from a battle. This was the work of someone who had deliberately wanted to create chaos. Drawers were pulled open, the sliding closet door taken off its track and clothing strewn everywhere and torn into rags.

Riley did a search of his own. He didn't expect to find anything. When Jenna entered the Witness Relocation Program, she'd had to leave all signs of her former life behind. There were no drawing pads, drawing pencils or paints lying around. A woman

who had been deemed an up-and-coming artist now
lived in an apartment that boasted no artwork on the
walls. He left the apartment as empty-handed as
when he'd entered.

Chapter 3

"Don't walk so fast," Jenna ordered, practically running to catch up with Riley's swift stride.

He frowned. "We're already running late. I don't intend to miss this flight."

"How can we go to Mexico? I'd need a visa."

Riley skidded to a stop and grabbed her arm in a firm grip. "This is not something to announce to the world," he stated between clenched teeth. "It's all taken care of. Visas are only necessary for extended stays. They'll only want ID when we leave the country."

"Well, pardon me, but I'm not used to acting like James Bond."

Riley looked at Jenna, dressed in an oversize T-shirt and tight jeans. With her shorter hair and big eyes highlighted, she looked as if she wasn't out of high school.

"Just be a good little girl and I'll let you have a soda on the plane."

Her eyes narrowed to mere slits. "You're so good to me, *Uncle, dearest.*"

Riley stared at his watch and swore under his breath.

He had wanted to reach the plane at the last minute, but they were cutting that last minute a little too short. He took Jenna's hand and practically dragged her down the airport's concourse.

"Fine, just pull me along like a piece of luggage," she muttered. "Just tell me something. Isn't Mexico a little obvious?"

Riley shot her a quelling look that effectively silenced her. His smile practically sizzled as he handed their boarding passes to the flight attendant. Not immune to his charm, she smiled back.

"You just made it, sir," she murmured.

"Thanks."

Once on board, Riley almost pushed Jenna into the window seat in first class before taking the seat next to her. He smiled at the flight attendant who handed him a glass of wine.

"Would the young lady like anything?" she asked, keeping her smiling gaze fastened on Riley's. Obviously she cared more about what Riley wanted than what Jenna wanted.

Jenna's smile could have frozen hell as she looked up at the attendant.

"A diet soda, please."

Jenna offered a brief smile as the attendant handed her her drink. She started to reach out with her right hand until she realized it couldn't hold anything. She quickly switched to her left hand.

Her cold smile transferred to Riley. "You call taking me across the border hiding me?" she whispered.

"It's called hide in plain sight," he murmured once the attendant had moved on, pulling a magazine out of the seat pocket and opening it. "They'll expect you to run for it, but they'll think you'll go east or west. Maybe even north to Canada. Mexico is too obvious."

Jenna slumped in her seat and studied her nails. The deep bloodred polish wasn't something she would have chosen for herself, but Sassy insisted it was part of her disguise. Sassy had even decorated her bandages with colorful sayings and pictures. Jenna only had to look in the mirror to think she was back in high school.

She thought over the traumatic events of the past few days and wondered why she wasn't cowering in a corner screaming her head off. A picture flashed by in the back of her mind. Darkness mingled with pain, a man's velvety voice promising even more pain. The plastic glass trembled violently in her hand.

Riley took it out of her hand and set it on the pull-down table in front of him.

"Flashbacks are expected," he murmured, taking her hand between his own. "All you can do is go along for the ride. They'll taper off after a while."

"Better a flashback than the real thing again." She wanted nothing more than to close her eyes and sleep. By sleeping, she could hope she'd wake up and discover all of this was just a horrible nightmare.

His hand tightened around hers. Not hard enough to hurt, but to remind her he was there.

As she looked at him out of the corner of her eye, she noted the dull green cotton shirt tucked into tan chinos. The sleeves were rolled up to reveal dark bronze forearms dusted with brown hair tipped with gold from the sun. Aviator-style sunglasses were slipped into his shirt pocket to add to the picture. With his hair tied back with a leather thong and the way he'd unobtrusively scan the passengers, he made a dangerous looking picture. She wasn't surprised the flight attendant kept giving Riley her best come-hither looks. There was something about dangerous men that women found attractive. A part of her wanted to explain none too politely to the woman that he was taken. Another part reminded her she'd given up that right when she entered the Witness Relocation Program.

She slumped down in her seat. Maybe she could go to sleep after all. And if she was lucky, she could wake up to find out she was back in her old life again.

Riley noted Jenna's sleeping form and requested a pillow and blanket. He carefully shifted her to a more comfortable position and slid the pillow under her cheek. He tucked the blanket around her and sat back so he could stretch out his legs.

He hadn't realized how easy it would be to return to his old way of life.

How many witnesses had he looked after? How many criminals had he tracked down and brought to justice? How many prisoners had he run to ground? Some had even given him interesting memories.

The well-known forger who escaped prison and was caught when he misspelled a name on a check.

An embezzler who lost the map to where he'd hidden the money he'd stolen. Lost it where the authorities could find it and not only find it but track him down, too.

Dealing with Grieco wasn't an interesting memory. The bastard was the reason Riley and Jenna had parted. Grieco and another madman, Leonard Randolph, were the kind of memories he wished he could erase.

The thing was that right now, he wasn't transporting a prisoner or tracking one down. He was protecting a witness. One who had ties to him—strong emotional ties. Toward the end of their time together, he'd even walked around carrying a ring, in the hope that he would get up the courage to ask her to marry him. Hoping, too, that he'd get over his feelings about starting a family. When she'd entered the Program without a thought about him, he'd put the ring away and never looked at it again.

He had thought he'd successfully put Jenna out of his mind. At least, he hadn't thought of her first thing in the morning and the last thing at night. Not in the past six months, anyway.

Now he sat next to her. Breathing in the soft scent of her skin. Hearing the barely there murmurs she made as she slept. His fingers itched to touch her. His body clamored to reclaim her.

He swore under his breath and pushed the call button. Whiskey wouldn't erase his feelings, but it would help numb them. Riley didn't want to pretend the past few years hadn't happened. He needed to keep his distance. It would be the only way he could keep her alive. He reminded himself Jenna wanted a family he couldn't give her. That, he tried to assure himself, was enough to keep him away from her.

Jenna felt groggy as she was rudely awakened when the jet made a less-than-comfortable landing in Mexico City. She was unceremoniously hustled off the jet by Riley and across the terminal to another gate.

"Excuse me?" She snatched her hand out of his grip.

"What?" He scowled down at her.

"I'm not getting on another plane until I use the ladies' room." Without another word she picked up her tote bag and headed off. She didn't have to look behind her to know Riley had followed.

Jenna splashed cool water on her face to help soothe the fatigue that had been plaguing her since she'd awakened. Grimacing at her reflection, she combed her fingers through the tangles. She reached into her tote bag for her lipstick and blush. Jenna wasn't going back out there without a touch-up.

When she stepped out of the rest room, she found Riley standing across the walkway, his back against the wall and one leg bent with the foot planted against the wall. A cigarette dangled from his lips.

His gaze was hooded as he watched her walk toward him.

"Our flight is boarding," was all he said as he

took her tote bag from her and pulled their boarding passes from his shirt pocket.

"Where are we going?"

"Don't worry, you'll like it."

"We're not talking the middle of the jungle, are we?"

"No jungle. Few bugs. Indoor plumbing."

"I guess that means I won't have to haul water from the river for my bath."

Once on the plane, Riley again had Jenna take the window seat while he sat by the aisle. This time he settled back and closed his eyes. He was asleep before the plane took off.

Jenna rummaged through her tote bag for one of the paperback books she'd found in there and began to read. She had noted each of the passengers boarding the plane but couldn't find anyone who looked remotely dangerous. She decided if Riley felt comfortable enough to sleep, she could relax and read. Although relaxing wasn't high on her list. She didn't want to think about lowering her guard when she was in a country where she couldn't speak the language and her life was in mortal danger. Only one man stood between her and death. She knew with Riley protecting her, the odds were in her favor. But it still didn't stop the fear from taking over when she least expected.

The words on the page ran together. She exhaled a sigh and closed the book. She glanced at Riley. He was slouched in his seat with his legs stretched out in front of him. Sitting in the front row allowed him the extra legroom. His chin rested on his chest and his arms were crossed in front of him.

He hadn't shaved that morning, and with his casual clothing and sunglasses propped on his nose, he looked as dangerous as a jungle cat.

Jenna thought of the first time she'd seen him.

He was wearing a pair of disreputable jeans and a gray sweatshirt with the sleeves chopped off to reveal the tattoo of a hawk on one upper arm. He'd spent the evening playing basketball with kids who would be ignored by most adults.

When her date had left her stranded on the side of the road, he'd been there to rescue her.

Her knight in worn denim and gray fleece.

Jenna's imagination had gone overboard in seeing him the way she'd wanted to. Now she was afraid to fall in love again with this man who lived in constant danger.

They were too different. She had grown up in rarefied air that involved the arts. She'd been touted as an up-and-coming artist. Her friends drew pictures, not guns.

Then Riley came into her life, and suddenly she was attending football and basketball games. He taught her how to play cutthroat miniature golf. She taught him backgammon. He taught her an afternoon in the park watching a game of touch football was fun, but participating in the game was even better. She taught him museums didn't have to be boring.

He taught her body to know his by the slightest touch. She taught him drinking champagne while lazing in the tub was better than drinking beer. He taught her just what sizzling passion was. She taught him to see the colors in a sunset.

Except she hadn't been able to teach him that family life could be enriching. He saw the bad side of life, while she looked for the good. He saw dark; she saw light. It hadn't stopped her from falling in love with him. It hadn't stopped her from hoping they might find a way to meld their differences into a winning combination. Then Grieco entered her life, and any chance she and Riley might have had was cruelly taken away.

Even now she wanted to reach over and touch him. She wanted to feel the warmth of his skin and feel the reassurance she knew she could experience just by laying her hand on his arm.

Except she no longer had that right. She'd given that up the day she'd entered the Program and left him behind.

I didn't want to leave you, Riley. Please believe me. I couldn't allow you to give up your career for me. It was too important to you. You could still do so much good that you wouldn't be allowed to do if you'd gone with me. She stared at him as if begging him to hear her thoughts.

"Is your book that boring?" His lips barely moved.

She jumped at the unexpected sound of his voice.

"I thought you were asleep," she murmured.

"It's easier to see what's going on around you if people don't think you're watching them."

"Of course." Jenna opened her book again.

"We've got about another hour in the air. Why don't you ask the attendant for something to drink."

"Where are we going?" she asked in a hushed voice.

A faint smile touched his lips. "Let's just say

we're going to a place where no one would expect
us to go.''

Jenna looked at him quizzically, but it was clear
he wasn't going to say any more on the subject.

The flight ended up being three hours, due to bad
weather. By the time the plane landed, Jenna was
exhausted and queasy from the bumpy travel.

She visibly drooped as she followed Riley off the
plane and into the small terminal. The air was so
humid her clothing stuck to her skin within minutes
and she could feel sweat trickle down her back.

She leaned against him as they waited for their
baggage. She was exhausted and felt ready to drop.
Riley gathered up their two suitcases and guided her
outside.

"When do we get there?" Jenna asked, aware she
sounded whiny. She was so tired she didn't care if
she sounded that way. She just wanted to be at a
place where the scenery didn't move around her. She
wanted a hot shower and a soft bed.

"Soon." He gestured to a taxi driver and after a
rapid exchange in Spanish, herded her into the car.

Jenna moaned when the small car took off at the
speed of light. Riley curved his arm around her
shoulders to steady her as the car raced around one
sharp curve then another. She turned her head and
buried her face against Riley's shoulder. He chuckled
softly in her ear as he tightened his hold on her.

"Don't worry, I'm sure he's made this trip hun-
dreds of times. I didn't see any scratched fenders.''

"There's always a first time," she mumbled

against his shirt. "If we're going to fall off a cliff, I don't want to see it coming."

She remained in that position for the next hour until the taxi finally screeched to a stop.

Riley reached into his pocket and pulled out some money. "We're here."

Jenna feared she looked like a zombie as she stumbled out of the taxi. A young man ran out of the hotel and took their bags from the driver. She looked upward but saw no name on the front of the building. Riley took her hand and guided her inside.

She was too exhausted to bother examining her surroundings or the people in the lobby, who were covertly watching them. She didn't really care who or what was there. All she cared about at the moment was lying down and sleeping for a week.

She stood by numbly as he conversed with the desk clerk. A moment later he was given a key, and a bellman led them out of the lobby. Soft lights marked a stone path that zigzagged ahead of them.

The bellman took them to a comfortable looking bungalow. After pointing out the bedroom, he turned on the light in an adjoining room and told them about the tub's whirlpool feature.

"Where are we?" Jenna asked, dropping onto a chair. She traced the Aztec pattern of the brightly colored cloth.

"A very nice resort where we can't be easily found," Riley answered once the bellman had left. He pushed open the bathroom door and went inside. "Trust me, you'll love it here. They've even got a spa, and there's a doctor on call if your hand starts bothering you. All the comforts of home and then some.''

Jenna shook her head, but the fuzzy feeling refused to go away. She was trying to sort out his words, but they kept getting jumbled.

''We're at a spa?''

''Not exactly.'' Riley set Jenna's bag on the luggage rack. ''I suppose you want the shower first.''

She pressed her fingers against her temples. A headache was now warring with her nausea.

Riley's hand covered her shoulder. ''Are you all right?''

Jenna shook her head. She looked up with eyes that were now a shimmering hazel courtesy of colored contact lenses.

''Am I all right? I'm about as far from all right as one person can be. I have been attacked, my life threatened, my own self turned into another person, and to top it all off, I've been on a jet, a plane that was probably built during World War I, then risked my life riding in a taxicab driven by a wild man. Now I find out I'm staying in a hotel on the edge of nowhere. How do you think I feel?'' She was close to tears.

Not wanting to break down in front of him, she brushed aside his hand and stood up. She wanted nothing more than the security of the bathroom with the door locked.

She didn't go more than one step before Riley's arms closed around her. With her face once again buried against his shirt, she could inhale the musky scent of his skin and feel the rasp of his beard-roughened chin rub gently against her forehead.

''It's been a hell of a lot more than you expected,

hasn't it, Smitty?'' he asked huskily. "But you need
to be kept safe. This was the only place I could think
of that was far enough away without our needing a
passport or visa.''

"And everyone hides out in Mexico, don't they?''
she choked out the words.

"Something like that, yes. I was down here once
on an undercover assignment to help track down an
escaped prisoner who was working as a waiter.'' He
kept rubbing his chin against the top of her head in
a soothing gesture. "This is a honeymoon resort.
They tend to take privacy to the nth degree. The hotel
is built up against a rocky cliff with a sheltered bay.
They have a couple of five-star restaurants, a fitness
center, a spa, swimming pool and a private beach.''

She sighed. "So what you're saying is we're here
on our honeymoon.''

"Exactly. We're here as Ryan and Jennifer Davidson. I doubt we'll run into all that many other
guests, anyway. As you can guess most of them prefer privacy.''

"Amazing,'' she murmured, so tired she was understanding little of what he was saying. She pushed
herself away from the warm comfort of his body before she gave in all the way and just stayed there.
"I'm going to take a shower.''

"Don't forget to use that plastic bag to keep your
cast dry,'' he called after her.

She went into the bedroom and deliberately ignored the king-size bed as she pulled some things
from her suitcase and carried her tote bag into the
bathroom.

Within moments, Riley could hear the faint sound
of the shower drumming against tile walls.

He felt the weariness deep within every bone in his body. Pouring himself a whiskey, he knocked it back in one gulp. The liquor burned its way down his throat and into his stomach. It did nothing to ease his fatigue, other than remind him he hadn't eaten anything for some hours. He sat back in the chair Jenna had vacated and closed his eyes.

He hadn't planned on bringing her here. Actually, he hadn't planned anything other than getting her out of Kansas City as fast as possible. It wasn't until he looked at the damage in her apartment that he knew he had to take her to somewhere where he felt he could keep her safe.

Without looking, he reached for the bottle and poured himself another drink.

He should order some food for both of them. Especially for him before the alcohol took effect.

He had to make sure Jenna was perfectly safe, so he shouldn't be drinking in the first place. He shouldn't have come back. He should have insisted he was out of it and stayed on his beach.

It took him a few minutes to realize the shower had stopped.

Riley pushed himself out of his chair and headed for the bedroom. "How about some dinn—" He stopped in the doorway and stared at the scene before him.

Jenna lay under the covers with her still-damp hair fanned across the pillow. Exhaustion was etched in her features as she slept.

Riley muttered a curse.

He was there to protect her. But who would protect him?

Chapter 4

"**H**ave you found them yet?" The man's voice was so sharp it could have cleanly sliced skin and not left a drop of blood behind. He sat behind his desk looking like an evil potentate, with a Cuban cigar in one hand and a glass of whiskey in the other. The only light in the room was a desk lamp that cast a mellow light on a face that could only belong to the devil.

"Not yet, but we're working on it." The man stood before the ornate walnut desk. He wasn't asked to sit. But then he never was. He was to stand there and listen to orders that were expected to be carried out without complaint. If they weren't…well, that was something he didn't think about. "I don't think it will take us long to find him."

That wasn't easy to do when you were tracking a man who could slip the most tenacious tail. He wasn't about to tell his employer that.

"I don't pay you to think. I pay you to do my bidding. Remember that."

He slowly puffed on his cigar as he regarded his employee with eyes that displayed no soul. If the other man had been superstitious he would have called on God for help.

"Yes, you will find both of them. Because if you don't..." He didn't need to finish his statement. It was well known what would happen if his wishes weren't carried out.

The man could feel perspiration gather in his armpits and trickle down his sides.

"You did an excellent job with the woman. It brought him to us. Unfortunately he left before we could meet again." His eyes turned cold. "Do whatever is necessary." The words were spoken in a low, menacing voice. "I don't want to see you again until you have carried out my wishes."

He nodded and quickly left the office. If he were smart, he'd get away as far as he could, but he knew he wouldn't remain free for long. The man he worked for had a very long reach. There was no doubt in his mind the day would come when he would die for not fulfilling his duty, unless he made sure to always do what he was told.

Jenna's sleep was soft and warm like a fluffy blanket. She was reluctant to wake up when her sleep-filled world was so lovely. She pulled the covers up over her head with the intent of drifting back to that fleecy white cloud.

Then her nose caught a rich familiar scent that

urged her to open her eyes. She did just that and saw a coffee cup sitting on the nightstand. She snuck one hand out from under the covers and touched the cup with her fingertips. It was still hot.

She sat up and reached for the cup. One sip turned to two then three as the caffeine flooded her system with a wake-up call.

"Think you can handle some food to go with the coffee?"

She turned her head and found Riley standing at the end of the bed. He looked disgustingly alert. His hair had a damp sheen from a recent shower, and he'd shaved. His faded navy cotton shorts and oatmeal-colored T-shirt probably weren't any different than any man would wear, but somehow on Riley the nondescript clothing looked sexy.

"Scrambled eggs, sausage, Belgian waffle," he intoned in a voice that was meant to tempt. "Danish pastries."

Jenna's mouth watered at the sight of the feast. She immediately sat up and started to swing her legs around to get out of bed.

"Uh-uh." Riley held up his hand to stop her. He returned to the parlor and came back with a tray in his hands. "Here you go, champ. A little bit of everything."

As Jenna sat back against the headboard, she noticed the dent in the pillow next to her. She was positive the dent had been made by Riley's head. The twinkle in his eye verified her suspicions.

"You were sound asleep," he confirmed, without a trace of apology. "And there's only one bed. The couch is only made for people under five feet tall."

Jenna scooped up a forkful of egg instead of speaking. She didn't want to admit the idea of his sleeping beside her was arousing.

"What's on the agenda for today? Brunch, perhaps some bodysurfing? Just an average vacation for an average couple."

Riley grinned at the sound of her tart words. "I can't say I'd call us average. After all, we are on our honeymoon."

"Well, that's true."

"You started it." He walked over and sat down on the bed. "About six steps outside the French doors is our own pool and spa. Every bungalow has a small private pool for its residents."

She shook her head, unable to take it all in. "Sounds like paradise."

"Close enough," Riley said. He leaned over and stole a corner of a raspberry pastry. "It's suitable for our purposes."

"Do you realize that in the past couple of days you've said the most you've ever said about your work?" she commented. "I had no idea about the details of what you did, other than what I saw watching news reports on television or watching movies."

Riley made a face regarding the latter. "Don't believe what you see on film, Smitty. Directors like to show us jumping out of burning buildings, or planes blowing up all around us. I don't think that happened once during my career."

Jenna tore off a piece of pastry and tossed it in her mouth. She should have felt odd, sitting in bed eating breakfast while Riley sat on the end of the bed. After all, for the past three years, she'd woken up alone.

Today brought back memories of mornings when he used to go out for a morning run and return with pastries or bagels and coffee. She remembered how he always teased her, saying the smell of fresh-brewed coffee was better than any alarm clock to wake her up after she'd had a long night waitressing at the restaurant.

The only difference between then and now was that she was wearing a nightgown this morning.

"What a shame you missed out on so much excitement," she drawled. She shot him a faintly accusing glare when he stole the rest of the pastry. "Did you not eat breakfast?"

He grinned, not looking the least bit guilty at getting caught. "Sure, I did. But I'm hungry again."

Jenna pulled her tray closer to her. "Then find your own food. This is mine."

For a moment, as she looked at him, she felt a tingle of electricity streak down her spine. The heated expression in his eyes had nothing to do with hunger for food, but for something much more elemental.

It would have been so easy for her to set the tray aside and silently let him know she wanted him as much as he wanted her.

Except too much had changed since the last time they'd been together. She had been forced to teach herself to adjust to an entirely different way of life. All of her past had been locked away in the back of her mind where she refused to allow it to surface. She refused to remember what it had been like.

Nor did she want to think of what happened between them the last night they were together.

She never forgot his anger at finding the pregnancy test. Or forgot his fury at what he'd felt was her betrayal. He had taken his share of the blame, but he still saw her as the one who'd tried to change their lives into something he had no desire for.

That last night was still a blur to her. Her fear of what she'd overheard had pretty much overridden everything else. There was Riley's stern demeanor as a marshal when he listened to what she had to say. He hadn't wasted any time in calling the authorities after she told him what she'd heard.

Within a half hour, two marshals showed up at her door, one a woman, and she'd left with them. She only saw Riley a few times after that. She was later told it was thought best they be kept separated during the trial.

She ached during all those torturous months, but she also did a lot of thinking. She had loved Riley with all her heart. With him she felt complete. And she felt he loved her even if he never said the words. If there was anything dividing them it was the issue of children.

Riley knew Jenna wanted her future to include children. He also made no bones that children weren't a part of his future.

That was why she had taken their relationship a day at a time. She'd never pushed for more, because she was happy just to be with him. She always felt if they were destined to be together for always, it would happen.

Then she realized destiny wasn't on their side— she went one way; Riley went another.

In time the wounds caused by parting with Riley

healed. She took her time carving out a niche where she could be comfortable. She had no desire to find love again. Willingly she'd given her heart to Riley and never wanted it back. After a time she was past caring. She had nothing left within her to give to another man.

After three years' separation, here they were together again. Except this time, their close quarters were not of their choosing. There wasn't a strong desire to be alone. They hadn't stolen away to a secluded resort because they'd wanted to escape the outside world for a while.

They'd fled because her life was in danger.

He hadn't come with her as her lover but as her protector. She hadn't missed the handgun tucked securely in his waistband so it would rest against his spine. She had no idea how he was able to bring it into the country. To be honest, she didn't want to know. She knew he carried it because of her. Before, he'd always kept his weapon in a locked box when he was home with her. She knew he wouldn't hesitate to use it.

She knew she should be even more scared than she was before. The man had beaten her badly, and she feared he would have killed her if it hadn't been for her neighbor's intervention. She knew as long as she was with Riley, she would be kept safe.

Jenna set the tray to one side and climbed out of bed.

"I'm taking a shower," she announced, picking up her coffee cup and carrying it with her into the bathroom. Before she closed the door, she glanced back at Riley. "What next, Mr. Cooper? Shuffle-board or golf?"

"Honeymooners have a habit of staying in. Wouldn't that be more believable?"

She ignored his wicked grin that still did strange things to her insides. "Not all honeymooners want to be alone twenty-four hours a day."

"Okay. How about a few sets of tennis?"

She raised her eyes heavenward. She was an admitted klutz where tennis was concerned. And he knew it. "I don't think so." She closed the door.

Riley waited until the door was securely closed before he started to reach for the last pastry.

"If you value your life you will not touch that last raspberry Danish!" The shouted command froze his stance.

"Damn, she's good," he muttered, getting off the bed and away from temptation.

Jenna swore under her breath as she struggled with the cast while using the hair dryer with her other hand. Sassy had promised her her hair would need little work other than a few swipes with the hair dryer and a brush. Except Jenna couldn't use both hands at the present time.

Once finished, she peeked out to see if Riley was still in the bedroom. Since it was empty she quickly ran out, gathered up underwear and clothing and ran back into the bathroom to get dressed.

She'd chosen a pair of yellow cotton shorts and a matching T-shirt with a modernistic fish design embroidered on the front since it seemed to suit the sunny day. Fed up with her hair, she'd finally pulled it up and back with a butterfly clip so only wisps gathered around her cheeks.

Jenna looked in the main room but didn't see Riley. She was ready to call out when she heard a familiar voice.

"Out here."

She turned around and went out through the open French doors. She put her hand over her eyes, shading them from the strong sun.

Riley sat in a wrought-iron chair he'd pulled up to the stone wall, his legs stretched out before him, feet propped on the wall. Sunglasses covered his eyes, and one of his hands held a glass. The contents looked like orange juice. He cocked an eyebrow at her as she sat on the wall facing him.

"Interesting color for you."

She looked down. "True, it wasn't something I would have worn before. But I'm learning there are a lot of things I didn't do before."

She could have sworn his gaze lingered on her cast.

"How does your hand feel?"

She looked down at her hand. She didn't even try to wiggle fingers that were still badly discolored and swollen.

"I don't have to take the heavy-duty painkillers anymore, so I guess that's a plus." She turned her head and looked out.

Below she could see the hint of a patio and pool identical to theirs. Farther out she could see the white sandy beach and a bay of shimmering blue water. Sand chairs dotted the beach, most of them filled with bronzed bodies. She could see some people bodysurfing in the waves.

She thought of so many mornings she had gone for a run on the beach to clear the cobwebs from her mind. Other mornings she and Riley ran together. Sometimes they would eat breakfast at a beachwalk café or return to her loft apartment to shower together and have breakfast before she escaped to her easel on mornings she didn't have to work and Riley left for work.

At that time, she had no idea what his work involved. She knew he was a U.S. Marshal and that there were times his work was dangerous. But he never brought his work home, and she knew enough not to ask about it. It hadn't mattered. She learned more than she wanted to when she entered the Relocation Program.

Why hadn't Riley stayed with the Marshal's Service?

She knew back then she couldn't ask about him, so she contented herself with the knowledge he was still doing the work he loved.

She turned around and leaned back against the wall.

"Why did you quit the Marshal Service?"

Riley stared forward, still sipping his juice.

"I decided I needed a quieter way of life." He turned, his eyes boring deep into hers. "Of course, you didn't bother to find that out, did you?"

Jenna's eyes narrowed as she stared back at him. He may have looked intimidating as hell, but she didn't feel the least bit unsettled. Riley would just have to learn she wasn't the cream puff he once knew.

"I don't believe I was given much of a choice back then. What I recall was receiving an order to pack a bag. I lived in a hotel for a while, and after the trial I was told to just forget my old way of life."

The smile on his lips wasn't reassuring. "Sweetheart, you had the choice to say no," he drawled with more than a hint of sarcasm.

"Of course. Enter the program or be killed by one of Grieco's men. Such a lovely choice, don't you think?"

Her biting tone didn't deter him one bit. This time, dark amusement lifted his lips. "Yeah. They still managed to find you, though."

Jenna's uninjured hand lifted an inch, but Riley didn't move. In the end, her fingers curled inward and her hand dropped back to her side.

"Yes, they did. But even in the beginning, I knew I had to do what was right." She didn't flinch from his searing gaze. "And even if I knew then what I know now, I'd do it again."

Confident she'd hit a nerve, she turned and walked back into the bungalow. The French doors were closed behind her.

Riley swore long and profusely under his breath as he set his glass down. "You idiot. You have the subtlety of a jackhammer," he berated himself, spinning around to face the view.

His first inclination was to march in there and just have it out with Jenna.

There was no doubt she harbored hostility over his leaving the service after she entered the Program.

Hell, he was the one who should be hostile! He had been putting his plan to resign into place when he learned she'd already entered the Program.

He had been able to talk to her a couple times on the telephone, but she never gave any indication what she planned to do. Not one hint. All he knew was that she wasn't there one day. She hadn't even left him a note to say goodbye.

Dave told him Jenna wanted it that way. She didn't want Riley to give up his career for her. Riley was hurt and furious. He handed in his badge and took off for a lonely shore.

He'd lived on scotch and cigarettes for the first two months. Then he'd woken up one morning with a mouth that tasted as if it had been filled with cow dung and a brain that felt as if it had been taken apart and put back together wrong.

Furious with himself for falling into a dark abyss of self-pity, he threw out the last of the scotch and locked the cigarettes away. It took him several months to clean out his system, and he felt like hell the entire time.

But he didn't give in, and afterward he felt it was worth it. It took him even longer than that to banish other runs on the beach as he headed out early each morning. But he did it.

Riley was a stubborn man. He did whatever was necessary.

Riley stayed outside for as long as he could. He wanted to give Jenna time to cool off. Not to mention he wanted some time to tamp down his own temper.

He muttered a few choice curses under his breath

as he pulled open the French doors and stepped inside. It took him less than thirty seconds to realize the bungalow was empty.

"Damn her," he swore as he tore out of the building and down the stone-covered path that led to the main building. Riley's grim features would have scared off most people.

His search of the hotel and shops only told him where Jenna wasn't. He learned she hadn't asked for a taxi, therefore she had to be in the vicinity still. His gut churned out acid the longer she remained out of his reach.

By the time he walked down to the beach, his head was pounding like an orchestra playing Beethoven's 1812 Overture and his stomach felt as if it was eating itself inside out.

The sun may have been warm and the day beautiful, but he could have cared less. What had his attention now was the musical sound of laughter. Jenna's laughter.

Then he saw her.

Resplendent in a tangerine-colored bikini, she reclined on a lounge chair as if she didn't have a care in the world. She had somehow twisted her hair up and held it with a clip that allowed loose strands to fall by her cheeks and against her nape. Dark-lensed sunglasses covered her eyes, and she was engrossed in a conversation with an elderly man who sat on the adjoining lounge chair.

Riley felt his jaw lock as he was positive the man was practically devouring Jenna with his eyes. He could have easily killed the man with his bare hands.

Instead, he took a deep breath and walked forward with a slow, sure pace.

"I still cannot believe the best Yorkshire pudding can be found in Singapore," Jenna said.

"If you wish, I can prove it to you by personally escorting you to the restaurant." The man spoke with a heavy Russian accent.

"Thank you for the invitation, but I don't think my wife would care to travel so soon after arriving here," Riley said with forced cheerfulness. The gaze he sent Jenna was a promise to hash this out later. The gaze he offered the other man was one that informed him Jenna was his property and his alone.

The older man smiled and nodded. "I have been having a lovely conversation with your wife. She has been kind enough to keep me company." He held out his hand. "I am Sasha."

"Ryan Davidson." He could tell by the older man's grip he was still strong.

"I understand you just arrived here," Sasha commented.

Riley nodded. "I'd heard about the resort and thought it might make a nice getaway." He laid a possessive hand on Jenna's shoulder as he sat down next to her on the lounge chair.

Her bare hip, warm from the sun, rested against his thigh. He threaded his fingers through hers, bringing her trapped hand to his knee and keeping it there.

Sasha's dark eyes scanned Jenna's relaxed posture, seeming to count each fading bruise on her bare skin.

Jenna made a face. "I told Sasha about my being mugged at the airport," she spoke the lie easily.

"And how I was so afraid it was a bad omen until you caught the mugger."

"It is sad thing when a lovely woman is harmed, is it not?" Sasha said to Riley. His weathered features seemed to ask many questions not said aloud.

"It is, but the mugger was caught and dealt with." Riley's expression also held unspoken words.

The older man smiled briefly and nodded. "That is good to hear." He glanced at the linked hands. "You are lucky to have your lives ahead of you. Unfortunately, I am only left with memories. But I have eight grandchildren who are determined to keep me young."

"You are a lucky man," Riley said honestly. "Children keep the family name alive."

"Yes, they do." Sasha carefully raised himself up and pulled a toweling robe about his portly figure. He leaned over Jenna and took her free hand, dropping a kiss on it. "It has been a pleasure to meet you, Jennifer. Thank you for giving an old man a lovely morning." A hint of the rogue he once was twinkled in his eyes as he looked at her, then turned to Riley. "Good day." He walked off with slow careful steps.

Riley waited until Sasha was out of earshot before speaking. Luckily, no one else was nearby to overhear their conversation.

"Is there a reason why you are making this more difficult than it has to be?" he asked in a low voice just in case there were eavesdroppers.

Jenna tried to pull her hand free, but was powerless against his stronger grip.

"I didn't care to stay inside, and you yourself said I'd be safe here."

Riley could feel his jaw aching from the effort to keep from yelling at her.

"He was an old man, Riley," she said in a voice that urged him to be reasonable. "And we were out here in public. I doubt anything could have happened to me."

He took a deep breath. "That old man owns this resort. He escaped from Russia during the Cold War. Rumor has it the resort started out as a rundown hotel and he worked hard to build it up to what it is today. I'd say he's still a force to reckon with. I don't care if he says he's Father Christmas. You can't trust anyone."

Her eyes glistened with tears as she stared back at him.

"Why are you doing this?" she whispered, finally able to reclaim her hand.

"To tell you there are times when even a nice old man isn't what he seems," he told her in a hard voice. "I still feel you're safer here than anywhere else. But you also have to follow my rules. One of which is you are not to leave the bungalow without me. You do not talk to anyone and you keep to yourself."

Riley steeled himself against the tear rolling down her cheek. Ordinarily, he would have leaned forward and caught it with his tongue. This time he sat there, keeping to his tough-guy image.

"You can look at it that way, but I still see a lovely old man who adores his grandchildren." Her chin wobbled with emotion.

"I don't care if you see him as the pope. Just be careful what you say."

"Thank you for reminding me." Sarcasm dripped from each word. "Naturally there is no way I would have forgotten." She held up her injured arm for emphasis.

Riley stood up, opting to forget her sarcasm. "As long as you follow my rules, you'll stay alive." He held out his hand.

Jenna looked up at him for several moments before she accepted his hand. She rose up slowly and turned to pick up a semisheer scarf of tropical colors swirled throughout the fabric. She tied it nonchalantly around her hips. It hid little and accented what was there.

"I guess it's time for lunch." She started up the beach.

Riley felt his blood pressure rise alarmingly. Along with something else rising. Jenna's bikini highlighted pale gold skin, but it was the thong bottom that caught his attention.

"Jenna, one. Riley, zip."

Chapter 5

Jenna should have felt triumphant that she'd won this round with Riley.

Except she knew she hadn't done it with words. She had accomplished her goal by blatantly using her femininity. It wasn't a good victory in her mind. Not one she could savor.

When she found the barely there thong bikini in her bag she knew it was the perfect thing to wear to the beach.

Especially when she was so furious with Riley and wanted to do something that she knew would upset him. She knew he wouldn't appreciate her going off without him and especially going off wearing the brief bikini.

If she was honest with herself, she'd admit it wasn't all his fault. It was just easier to blame him since he was the closest target.

She wanted to hate him for taking control of her life. She admitted to herself that she was the one who'd kept asking for him, and she was the one who wouldn't talk until he showed up. She should have known he would be in charge all the way, without giving her a hint as to what he was doing.

Jenna thought she was at a point in her life when she was in control of her future. While she lived the past few years in a manner she'd planned, she had accustomed herself to a situation she couldn't control.

She hated the idea of being out of control. The worst was that horrific night when a man invaded her home and invaded her mind.

Her skin prickled uncomfortably as she stood under the shower spray. A sign she'd had too much sun this morning. After she dried off, she smoothed on lotion to ease the slight sting. The lightweight cotton sundress felt cool against her skin.

When she left the bathroom, she found Riley stretched out on the bed. The television was on showing a Western movie.

"The hotel has an excellent satellite dish," he said, explaining the reason for the English-speaking movie.

"Of course, they would," she murmured, moving over to a nearby chair. "Riley, I'm sorry I went off without leaving word this morning. Especially after all the times you'd warned me not to do just that. It's just that I'd finally gotten used to doing things on my own when it seemed everything turned upside down again."

He picked up the remote and hit the mute button. The sound on the television was instantly silenced.

"Which probably has you wishing you'd never met me in the first place," he stated without an ounce of emotion in his voice.

Jenna shook her head. "No, I've never regretted the time we had together. What I regret is—" She looked down at her hands. She gently ran her fingers over the hand still badly discolored from injuries. She swallowed and looked up. "Do you know how hard it is to stop yourself from even just doodling because those doodles turn into pictures? And you're afraid someone will notice the doodles and ask why you haven't considered drawing. How you can't look at a sunset because you'll feel the ache of not being able to paint it. Or the pain you feel because you can't even walk past an art supply store because it will be too tempting to go in. I had to concentrate on writing my new name. I had to remind myself that was the name I answered to and I had a new background to memorize. I had a beautiful loft." Her words were barely audible. "I left friends I'd known most of my life. I left behind everything I knew...and loved." Her lips barely moved as she spoke. "If I rebel now it's because I'm afraid of having my life spiraling out of control again. I'm afraid this time I won't be able to control it. That I'll never find me again."

"Why did you ask for me?"

Riley's abrupt question had her looking up. "What?"

"You heard me the first time. Why did you ask for me? Why did you insist I come to you? You had the marshal in charge of your case, and Dave was there. Why me?"

She rubbed the spot between her brows as if rubbing away past pain. "I was in shock, and I had no idea what was going on around me. No one talked *to* me. I needed something familiar. I chose you."

"You had to have known there was a chance I couldn't reach you immediately. You had two marshals there to handle everything necessary. You wouldn't have been in any immediate danger," he insisted. He wanted to know exactly why she called for him.

Jenna wrinkled her nose. "Obviously, you never dealt with Vince Cameron. I told them if they called Vince I would make a fuss like they'd never seen before. They didn't listen to me and called him, anyway."

"Vince Cameron? They put him in charge of your case?" Riley's voice rose with every word. "He couldn't handle relocating a cat much less a person. No wonder you ended up in the middle of the country. I, at least, would have put you in a city with a sizable lake in the vicinity."

Jenna chuckled. "It was the beach, not water in general that had my attention."

"That's why it was taken away from you. It was obvious they told you the rules when you entered the Program."

She nodded. "Of course. They were very thorough." She fidgeted with the hem of her dress for lack of anything better to do. "I understand Dave kept tabs on me, but I didn't learn about that until a

few days ago." She licked her lips. "How long will
we have to stay here?"

"Until I know you're safe. With all they're offering around here, I don't think you'll get too bored."

"Not good enough, Riley," she argued. "No one
knows who the man was. I wouldn't know him if he
stood in front of me. For all we know, he could slip
into the hotel and pretend to be a worker here."

Riley sat up in one graceful move and shifted
around to sit on the edge of the bed.

"Oh, I think you'd know him, Jen. There are ways
of recognizing a person other than what they look
like. I bet you'd recognize his voice if you heard it
again, wouldn't you?"

Riley's voice was soft, drifting through her mind
like a seductive mist. "He was there with you for
some time, wasn't he? He was there telling you what
he wanted to do to you. He said lots of things you
didn't want to hear. He wanted you afraid of him.
He wanted to inflict pain with every word he said."

With each word he spoke, Jenna's face turned
whiter. With each word her eyes grew larger and
darker as she stared at him. Horror stiffened her posture to that of a statue.

Riley hated to see her like this but he had to con-
tinue. "Did he keep on talking to you as he broke
your fingers, Jenna?" He kept his voice insidiously
quiet. "Did he tell you he wanted to make sure you
would never paint again? Did he say that was why
he was there? Did he keep you so afraid of him, you
couldn't utter a sound? That you were even afraid to
scream? You bit your lip to keep from screaming,

didn't you? And you kept on biting it until the pain grew so great you had no choice but to scream.''

"Stop it! Just stop it!" She jumped to her feet with her hands held over her ears to keep out the cruel sound of Riley's voice that brought back terrors she preferred be kept hidden. "I never want to hear his voice again! He was cold and he was cruel and he laughed every time he hurt me. I never want to hear that horrible laugh again.'' She kept her eyes open as if she knew closing them wouldn't block out the images but intensify them. "His hands were cruel and his voice horrible. He liked hurting people. He liked hurting me.''

"He told you that.''

She shook her head. She still refused to look at him. Her face flamed with color. "He didn't have to tell me. I could tell by the sound of his voice. By his body.''

Riley inwardly winced at the fear written so starkly on Jenna's face. He hated putting her through this, but he hoped he might be able to find out things others hadn't. He'd read the report. He'd seen what a small amount of information had been given by Jenna. It was assumed because the room was dark and the man wore a ski mask and gloves, she could give them little in the way of identification. And that the horror of that time had left her memory blank.

He knew better. Jenna had been an artist. A very talented one. She used all her senses in her work, which had always made it more special. He refused to believe she had closed off that part of herself. He had to consider she knew something, but had buried it deep within her memory, out of self-defense.

"Did he call you by name?" He knew some of the answers, but he still wanted to hear it in her words.

She nodded jerkily. She wrapped her arms around her body in an attempt to shield herself from the memories.

"Did he use your real name or did he call you by your new name?" he pressed.

"My real one," she whispered. "He used both names at first. He said he knew which one was my real one and seemed to enjoy using it more."

"What did his voice sound like?"

It took her several minutes to answer. Even then she could barely speak above a whisper. "Evil."

"Did he have an accent?"

Her brow furrowed in thought. "Not exactly."

His senses sharpened. "How not exactly?"

"He had trouble saying some words. Sort of like a speech impediment." Her hands jerkily moved over her face as if needing to assure herself she was all right and not back in the nightmare.

Aha. Something that hadn't been mentioned before.

Riley leaned forward. "What words, Jenna?"

She started to tremble. "I don't want to say them."

He could feel the muscles in his jaw tighten. "I need to know, Jenna."

She shook her head, the movement almost violent.

"I want to find the man." *And kill him for what he's done to you.*

Jenna didn't say a word. She just kept shaking her head.

"Tell me." He waited a beat. "Jenna, tell me the words." He remembered a hint of a stubborn streak, but it appeared to have strengthened over time. *"Tell me the damn words!"*

He didn't expect her to spin around and scream words that were so sick and twisted, they even filled him with disgust. Now he knew her temporary captor knew exactly how to frighten her and he did it well. When she finished, she dropped into the chair and buried her face in her hands.

Riley was off the bed in a flash. He crouched down in front of Jenna and carefully peeled her hands from her face. He wrapped his own hands around them, rubbing them briskly but was careful not to be too rough with her cast.

"Jenna. Jenna, listen to me," he said gently. "This bastard has to be found and you're the only one who can help me. Obviously, no one bothered to ask you the right questions. I know it hurts like hell and I know you don't want to remember what happened that night, but I need to know. The more I know the easier it will be to find him. What else was different about him?"

Jenna still refused to look at him. "He liked to rub himself against me," she murmured. "And he wanted me to touch him. But he never—" she gulped "—he never got aroused."

This time Riley closed his eyes. There was no denying she had been up against a sick bastard who enjoyed intimidating women.

"What about smell. Aftershave? Chewing gum? Breath mints? Anything there?" he asked.

She closed her eyes, then shuddered. Her eyes

popped open and this time she did look at him. "Baby powder. He wore gloves, but I could still smell baby powder on them." She looked surprised she'd remembered such a minor detail.

Riley nodded. "He wanted to keep his hands dry. Anything else?"

She closed her eyes, then opened them. "His breath smelled like licorice. As if he'd recently eaten some. Otherwise, he was cool, calm and collected. He didn't even sweat."

He muttered an oath under his breath. "He was a true professional. Nothing to give him away except for the baby powder and licorice. A couple of points most people might not remember. You told them you thought he was about six foot one, one hundred eighty pounds and all muscle."

She nodded.

"Good." Riley slapped his thighs and rose up. He reached out for her hand and pulled her to her feet. "I know you won't believe me, but talking it out will actually make you feel better. There won't be as many bogeymen in the closet for you to fear, because you're bringing them out into the open."

She tipped her head back to look up at him. "When you say he's a professional, you mean he was paid to do what he did. That he might come back again."

"He was a professional. He was paid to hurt you. Something tells me there's more to it than just terrorizing you. Yes, he will try to find you again," he said bluntly.

"Don't sugarcoat the news, Riley," she said sarcastically. "You're telling me the guy is the type to keep on looking until he finds me, and next time he might kill me." Her voice rose to a dismayed squeak.

"You don't need to worry. Because if he does manage to find you, he'll have to go through me, and that's exactly what I'd like him to do."

With those words, Jenna had a glimpse of the tough cop Riley must have been. She wasn't sure she cared to ever see it again.

He gently brushed her bangs off her forehead and guided her over to the bed. It didn't take much urging for her to lie down and relax. She was positive she'd never sleep again and even told him so. She was wrong. Within moments, she was sound asleep.

When she opened her eyes a couple hours later, her first sight was of Riley seated in the chair she'd been sitting in earlier. His fingers were pressed together in steeple fashion, his gaze looking at something she couldn't see. He smiled at her.

"It seems we both skipped lunch. How does an early dinner sound?" he asked, coming out of his self-imposed trance.

Jenna pushed her hair away from her face as she yawned. She sat up. "What time is it?"

"Almost five."

She swung around until she sat on the side of the bed. "I would think this resort believes in continental hours for dinner."

"The resort caters to all its guests—breakfast, lunch and dinner are offered around the clock. Rumor has it there's a kitchen for each meal," he explained.

Jenna tried to calculate the cost of staying in a resort that catered to the guests on such a royal level.

"How much is this costing?"

Riley grinned. "Don't worry, sweetheart, you don't have to come up with the scratch."

"Good thing, because our stay would have been over the moment we stepped inside the lobby," she said wryly. "You're lucky Sassy packed something appropriate for dining out."

"There wouldn't have been a problem if she hadn't. There are plenty of shops in the lobby for anything you need. Since we might be here for a while, you might want to do some shopping for a few more things to tide you over. Don't worry, all the costs are covered," he added.

Jenna shook her head. "Why would the government be willing to go to these lengths to protect me? Not to mention the expense. It's not as if I was an important witness in the first place. Steven Grieco might have been a criminal, but he wasn't on the top ten list. So why all this attention?"

Riley didn't say anything for a moment. He looked off in the distance, then turned back to her.

"What makes you think he wasn't all that important?" he asked in a soft voice.

She looked surprised by his question. "Why? Well, because he'd never been charged for anything before."

"Who told you that? The state's attorney?"

Jenna nodded uncertainly.

Riley's chest expanded as he breathed a deep sigh. "Jen, Grieco hadn't been charged before because he either bought someone off or made them disappear before any charges could be filed. He was a master at making witnesses disappear. If we hadn't moved as swiftly as we did, he would have made you disappear, too. Any crime boss worth his salt can still operate even while sitting in a Federal penitentiary. I'm not surprised that he put the word out to have you found. He probably did it as soon as his conviction came in. I admit I don't understand why it took so long. For now I'll just worry about the fact that they did find you.''

"All this began because I was in the wrong place at the wrong time," she murmured, feeling the cold shock of fear well up inside her again. She dragged her pillow toward her and hugged it tightly against her chest. "You're basically saying that his men could find me here. That man who found me before could turn up here." Her teeth started to chatter.

"He was very clever. He used your real name. He wasn't out to kill you, just badly frighten you. Which he did," he murmured under his breath. "He was playing with you, Jenna. The way a cat plays with a mouse. He could then sit back and wait awhile. He knew the authorities would be brought in and that was fine with him. He's probably a very patient man. He knows they'll relocate you and he'll be around to get an idea where you're going. That way he can attack you again. He'll want you to think that no matter where you go, he'll be there. He wouldn't want you to relax. His getting off on you being scared of him. Grieco chose the perfect person to terrorize you, because the man made sure you'll have nightmares for many a night. He's the kind of guy who wants you to be so afraid you'll welcome your death when he feels the time is right. He wants to be in charge, Jen. We're making sure that doesn't happen.''

"No safe haven. Always looking over my shoulder.'' The horror of that night was again reflected in her eyes. "Never sleeping well. Always having to be on guard. It's not a good way to live.''

"You're right, it's not,'' Riley agreed. "But it's a good way to turn an adult into a whimpering child afraid of their own shadow. He's a formidable opponent because he's very clever. Who knows how long he'd been staking you out before he struck.''

She couldn't sit still any longer. She jumped up and threw the pillow to one side. It bounced off the bed and fell to the floor unnoticed.

"You think he will follow me here. In fact, you hope so. I'm nothing more than a goat tied to a stake. As far as you're concerned, I'm nothing more than bait!'' In a furious fit, she stooped to pick up the pillow and threw it at him.

He easily deflected the soft missile.

"I may be a bastard at times, but I'm not that callous a bastard.'' He directed a level look her way. "If he does show up here, we'll have the advantage.''

"Oh really?'' Her tone dripped sarcasm. "And what advantage do *we* have?''

Riley grinned. "Because, Smitty, I'm teaching you to kick butt.''

Jenna wrinkled her nose. "I took a self-defense course, thank you very much. In case you can't tell, it didn't do me much good.''

He shot her a wry look. "That's because I wasn't the instructor."

"It must be hell to be so perfect."

He ignored her droll tone. "What I'm saying is, what I'll be teaching you is fighting you learn on the streets. You're going to learn to use your feet, your fingers, nails and elbows. You'll learn to fight dirty and use whatever is available to best your opponent."

Jenna stared at him, taking in the words. "I'll do whatever it takes."

Riley nodded. "Good."

He stretched his arms over his head. "I'm starved, and I'm sure you are, too. Do you want the shower first or shall I take it?"

"I'll take it." She swept past him as she walked to the dresser and withdrew articles of clothing. She walked into the bathroom and firmly closed the door behind her.

"And here I was going to ask if you'd care to share," he murmured. "I guess you wouldn't."

Riley realized his mistake the moment he stepped into the bathroom after Jenna vacated it. The air was still warm and steamy, fragrant with the scent she'd used on her skin. He felt as if she was wrapped all around him.

He found a large jar of body cream sitting on the counter and picked it up, opening it and sniffing the contents. The heady aroma of spice and vanilla brought back memories of lazy afternoons they'd spent in bed. He dipped a finger into the contents and rubbed it between his fingers. He thought it was specks of mica that had given his skin a sheen. He sniffed his arm. He preferred the fragrance on her skin.

He turned on the shower and stepped inside, shutting the glass door. By closing his eyes and gritting his teeth, he was able to withstand the icy water without swearing up a storm.

The last thing he wanted Jenna to do was know just how much she affected him.

A cop who couldn't keep his mind on his assignment usually ended up dead. And because of that inattention, his assignment would end up just as dead.

There was only one problem. He could never consider Jenna an assignment.

Chapter 6

"One of the restaurants offers terrace dining if you'd rather eat outdoors," Riley suggested as they walked toward the main building. "Or we can eat inside if that would make you feel more comfortable. One of the indoor restaurants has an aquarium along one wall, while the terrace restaurant is surrounded by a koi pond."

"I'm so hungry I feel as if I could eat a seven-course meal in the middle of a war zone."

When they entered the restaurant, Jenna learned Riley had understated its charm. The dining area was limited to ten tables, which were surrounded by a pond. Diners reached their table by crossing a small bridge where they could also pause to enjoy the colorful fish. Beyond the pond was the breathtaking view of the bay and sandy beach. The setting sun laid brilliant oranges and reds onto the blue water.

"This place is incredible," she said under her breath as they were escorted to their table.

"Sasha wanted his guests to feel as if they were in a home away from home," Riley replied once they were seated.

"He did a wonderful job, then."

"Ah, the lovely Jennifer." Sasha stopped by their table. A small boy wearing dark shorts and a red T-shirt stood next to him. "I am glad to see you didn't stay out too long in the sun. Many visitors forget how unforgivable the sun can be to those not used to it."

"I never enjoyed looking like broiled lobster. The suffering never seemed worth it." She smiled at Sasha then at the boy who offered a shy smile in return. "Is this your grandson?"

He nodded. "This is little Sasha." He placed his hand on the boy's shoulder. "His mother and father have sent him and his nanny down here to stay with me while they enjoy a second honeymoon."

"They're on a big boat," the little boy piped up.

Sasha chuckled. "They are taking a cruise in the Caribbean. Luckily, little Sasha preferred to come here with me than insist on going with his parents."

"Well, Sasha, I'd say you have a wonderful grandfather to wànt you to come down here and keep him company," Jenna told the boy.

He grinned. "I like it here because Grandpa lets me go swimming every day even if I don't eat my peas."

"The boy is spoiled," Sasha confided with a wry smile. "But he has eyes like his grandmother's, so I have no choice but to give in to him." He nodded at Jenna then Riley. "I will leave you to your dinner.

I hope you will enjoy all we have to offer here." He walked off with the boy holding on to his hand.

Riley didn't miss the hunger in Jenna's eyes as she watched the little boy.

Some things never changed, he told himself as he studied her profile.

Except Jenna's life had changed so drastically that she hadn't been able to fulfill her dream of having a child, and maybe she never would.

When she turned back to him, she had fixed her smile to be as open as if she didn't have a care in the world.

Except Riley knew better.

"Do you want to start with an appetizer?" he asked, pretending to study the menu. "The sampler plate sounds interesting and would give us a little of everything."

Jenna turned her attention back to the menu. She agreed with his suggestion and decided on the seafood buffet while Riley selected a steak.

"How can you choose steak when they have all this wonderful seafood available?" Jenna was incredulous after the waiter left them.

He shrugged. "What can I say? I hate fish."

Deciding to treat this time as a vacation, Jenna ordered a planter's punch. She wasn't surprised that Riley asked for beer. Although he did ask for an imported label.

"So what have you been doing in Kansas City?" Riley asked, after Jenna returned to the table with her plate filled with seafood delicacies.

She applied herself to her meal. "I'm sure my file told you everything you need to know."

"Maybe it did, but I didn't read it. I figured anything I needed to know, I'd hear from you."

"I've worked as a secretary to a grammar school principal for the past two years." She explained. "I took courses in computer and office skills to give me a start in my new life. I guess that kind of work wouldn't be considered exciting, but it paid the bills. And it kept me busy. I also took two night courses a semester. So far, some of my new skills involve Thai cooking, creating full meals using a Crock-Pot, calligraphy and then two ballet classes and a yoga class. I've also participated in some of the 5K runs the city has sponsored."

"What about a social life?"

She could feel his keen gaze practically dissecting her, but she didn't allow him to disconcert her.

"I don't think that part of my life is any of your business."

"Which means no," he stated.

"Which means you gave up the rights to ask me personal questions three years ago." She speared a piece of crab with her fork and brought it to her lips. She offered him a cool smile. "Just as I have no rights to question you about your personal life in regards to the past couple years."

She hoped her expression didn't reveal she was kicking herself for even bringing it up.

Her hopes were fruitless. Riley's reckless grin told her that.

But then he'd always known what was going on inside her head. She remembered times when she felt he knew her better than she did. Especially during intimate moments.

She concentrated on her food.

"You work during the day, night school two nights a week. What about the other five nights? The weekends you weren't running a 5K?" he persisted. "What did you do during all that free time?"

"I have already told you more than you need to know," she said frostily. "So why don't you be a good little caveman and eat your dinner?"

Riley merely chuckled, not the least bit deterred by her haughty tone, and settled back to eat his meal.

All through dinner he played the part of the adoring new husband. He was so perfect Jenna could easily have forgotten this was a ruse.

Jenna could find no fault with him as the perfect dinner companion. Even if she did want to hit him over the head with her plate.

She couldn't miss the presence of carefully masked desire in the air coming from the other diners. She looked around and saw couples eating, but she felt as if some of them had merely come up for air before returning to the privacy of their bungalows. A few were less discreet, and she wondered why they just didn't use room service.

"Amazing," she commented, picking up her glass of wine and taking a sip.

"What is?" he asked.

"Why bother having such lovely restaurants when it's obvious everyone here would prefer being alone," she commented.

Riley cocked an eyebrow. "Everyone, huh? Does that mean you want me to ask the waiter to have our meal sent to the bungalow?"

There was no mistaking the wicked gleam in his eye.

She smiled at him as if he were a charming little boy who'd said something precocious. But inwardly she couldn't help thinking about how the past few days had changed her way of seeing life: the trauma of her attack had left her feeling vulnerable at first; after a few days she'd started experiencing anger over her situation; she was now at the point where she realized that no matter how much protection she might have, she still needed to find the inner strength to take care of herself.

She knew the day would come when the man who attacked her would be caught. When that happened, she would be considered no longer in danger. She would be relocated to another city and state. Riley's assignment would be over, and he would return to the home he'd made for himself.

After the past three years she didn't dare hope she could find a way to convince him to stay with her. After all, she'd been the one who'd left him so abruptly the last time. What she had come to realize was that she didn't want to be alone any longer.

She told herself not to linger in self-pity any longer. No matter what it took she had to shore up her defenses. And she told herself she had to forget what it had been like when she and Riley had been together. She must not think about what he felt like under her fingertips. The way his skin smelled so warm and musky as her tongue outlined the ripcord muscles when they made love. The way...

She quickly snatched herself back to the present before her feelings were written on her face.

"Look at the size of some of those fish," Riley muttered, looking over at the pond. "Do you think they eat meat? I've heard there's some fish that will eat hamburger."

She forced herself to turn her head to look at the pond. "I don't see Jaws in there, so I guess it wouldn't hurt for you to dive in and find out."

Riley shot her his I-know-what-you're-trying-to-do-and-it-won't-work look.

Jenna smiled blandly. She pushed her plate to one side and stood up. "I'm going back for seconds."

"If they have any more of those little rolls, would you bring me a couple?" he asked.

She nodded and walked toward the bridge.

Jenna chose her food and placed several of the warm yeasty rolls for Riley on her plate. She was adding a few slices of melon to her plate when a man picked up a plate and stood next to her as he perused the buffet table.

"If your friend does not treat you right, please call Carlo. I am in bungalow twelve," he murmured as he walked past her.

Jenna didn't dare look after him. But she couldn't stop grinning as she returned to her chair.

"What did Mr. Miles of Smiles want?" Riley asked, as Jenna sat down.

She passed over a couple rolls to him then broke one of hers open, buttering it lightly.

"His name is Carlo and he's in bungalow twelve. He's hoping I'll stop by. Obviously, not everyone is here on a honeymoon." She used her fork to slice off a bite of melon. "He's a bit intense for my taste, but I told him I could just lock you in the closet and stop by for a drink.''

"And here I thought I was your main squeeze." He finished cutting his steak into bite-size pieces.

"Naw, I thought I'd find out if all the stories are true about Italian men," she said lightly.

"Hey, I could have told you the truth without you having to put yourself out. They're all lousy lovers."

"As if I'd believe you." She arched an eyebrow. "You were also the one who told me that the pot of gold at the end of the rainbow is really gold-foil-covered chocolate coins." The moment she said it, she wished she could take back the words. The mention of rainbows only brought back memories best stored away.

"You thought it was a good idea," he defended himself.

Jenna thought of the night she'd come home from work feeling so tired she only wanted to sleep. Instead, Riley had surprised her with a seduction and a rainbow sun catcher. She had cried when she had to leave it behind.

To this day she wondered what had happened to the sun catcher after she left. Arrangements had been made to sell the loft. But it was the loss of the sun catcher she mourned.

To keep up appearances, she speared a shrimp with her fork. For the life of her, she couldn't bring the succulent morsel to her lips. For the moment her appetite was gone. She finally managed to eat a few bites.

"Want to stop by the *lanai* bar for a while?" Riley asked her later after he'd signed the check. "We could sit there and listen to music. Maybe sip those rum drinks with colorful little paper umbrellas in the glasses.''

"Sure, why not?" She pushed back her chair and stood up.

Riley's hand rested possessively against her lower back as they left the dining area. Jenna made sure not to make eye contact with Carlo as she walked past his table. She didn't want to give the man any ideas.

"Why does a resort in Mexico give the pretense of being an exclusive resort you could find on any of the Pacific Islands?" she asked as Riley seated her at a table. "The wildlife fits in. Just not the decor." She nodded toward a large cage near the bar that housed two Greenwing macaws that chattered away much to the amusement of the guests. A small monkey sat perched on the bartender's shoulder where he also chattered away.

"Sasha just wants it to be paradise." Riley sat sprawled in his chair, one leg cocked with his ankle resting on his opposite knee. "Mexico's always been known as a poor country. Some areas are so poor that they can't even hide it from the tourists. Here you can feel as if you're in another world."

"Another world," she laughed softly. "I've been in another world for the past three years. Not a poor one except in life, itself." She picked up the pink paper umbrella that had come with her drink and twirled it between her fingers. "I have to say this one is much nicer."

"Because of the beach?"

She nodded, not surprised he easily picked up on

what would attract her the most. She knew just looking at the water had her recalling all the times she and Riley ran on the beach in the early morning hours and sometimes in the early evening. She always felt free when she ran on the hard-packed sand. She even felt she got some of her best ideas then.

She looked down at her injured hand that lay heavily in her lap. So far she had forced herself to ignore the cast. She made a face at the wild designs decorating it.

"I think Sassy got a little too enthusiastic with her artwork," she commented.

"She does have her moments," Riley agreed with a lazy smile. "They have a doctor here. I bet he could even replace the cast for you."

"You think so?" She showed her skepticism.

"Sure. I'm sure there's been a guest or two who's broken a bone." He gestured to the waitress, and after a brief conversation with her she returned with a cordless phone.

Jenna listened to him make his request. After he disconnected the call, he told her the doctor would be willing to see her in a half hour.

"I don't believe this." she laughed.

"I told you. This place delivers service with a smile." He lifted his drink in a toast.

Which is what Jenna discovered when she and Riley later headed for what was termed the infirmary, but looked more like the luxurious interior of a doctor's office in New York or Beverly Hills.

Dr. Minton was a tall, reed-slender man, who spoke with an upper-crust British accent.

He led them into an examination room that looked state-of-the-art with medical equipment. With the assistance of a nurse, he easily removed the cast. He suggested that they first X-ray Jenna's hand to see how it was. After pronouncing that the healing process was proceeding well, he informed her she wouldn't need a cast. He used a special bandage that would do the same thing without it being as cumbersome as a cast.

"This way you won't have to fear getting the bandages wet," he assured her as he wrapped her hand with a firm, sure touch. "You can also come in anytime when you require a new bandage. If you experience any discomfort I can prescribe some painkillers for you."

She shook her head. "To be honest, I haven't had all that much pain. Just some discomfort that extra-strength aspirin has taken care of without much trouble."

He nodded. "Well, if you do feel you require anything stronger, please feel free to call down here and I can give you something stronger."

"A resort in Mexico with a South Pacific theme and a bonafide British doctor who looks and sounds like James Bond," she told Riley after they'd left the infirmary. "Are you sure this isn't some kind of hideout for spies?"

"Not that I've heard of, but it would make for a good movie, wouldn't it?" He gently picked up her arm and inspected the pink bandage wrapped around her wrist and still-splinted fingers. "A very nice job. I wouldn't be surprised if you only needed minimal physical therapy."

Jenna spun around and began walking backward so she could face him. She occasionally looked over her shoulder to make sure there was nothing to trip over.

"Yes, Doctor, but will I play the violin again?" she asked in a mock-haughty tone. The full skirt of her dress billowed up around her thighs as the ocean breeze picked up.

Riley reached forward and grabbed her around the waist, lifting her off her feet so she wouldn't step on a lizard lazing on a warm stone in the walkway.

"Old joke, Smitty," he murmured, his breath warm against her lips as he still held her against him. "But I wouldn't worry. You'll do whatever you want to. I know you will."

The light in her eyes dimmed for a moment at the solemn note in his voice. She should have known she couldn't fool him. Her fingers were still bruised and slightly swollen. She couldn't miss the way they looked crooked. The doctor assured her they weren't crooked, but she had trouble believing him. All she knew was if they remained crooked, she couldn't hold a brush. And if she couldn't hold a brush, she would never have the chance to paint again.

"Don't make promises you can't keep, Riley."

Chapter 7

No matter what Jenna tried, she couldn't sleep.

The doctor's handling of her injured hand had been gentle and careful, but after a busy day she was experiencing just enough discomfort that sleep was beyond her. Not to mention she couldn't find a comfortable spot to sleep. She'd swallowed a couple of aspirin before she'd gone to bed in hopes they would help.

An hour later, she wondered if the aspirin had lost its effectiveness. She rolled over and nestled her cheek against her pillow, staring at the door leading to the parlor. She had partially closed it before she went to bed. It was open just enough that she could see a light streaming in. If she turned her head a little more, she could catch a glimpse of Riley seated in a chair. A book lay in his lap, and his head was tilted back against the chair.

Because it was so quiet, she could hear the soft sounds of his snores floating in the air. She smiled as the rough snorts reached her ears. While most people found snoring annoying, she'd always found his snoring comforting.

She wondered what he would say if she told him it had taken a long time for her sleep in complete silence.

She knew she should get up and wake him. She could urge him to come to bed where he could be more comfortable than sitting in that chair. It was certainly big enough for the two of them. Instead, she snuggled under the covers and fell back asleep to the sounds of Riley's soft snores.

The first thing Riley felt when he woke up was a nagging ache in his neck. The second hint that he felt like hell was another nagging ache along his right thigh. The third was a cramp that began at the bottom of his calf and moved upward. He gritted his teeth and struggled to decide which area of pain to take care of first.

"I'm too old for this crap," he muttered, wincing as he leaned forward to rub the cramp. Except the movement sent streaks of pain moving across his neck. "Damn!"

"And here I thought you could sleep as easily in a chair as you could in a bed. My, my, and I thought you were such a tough guy, too."

He paused in his internal diagnosis to glance up. He found Jenna standing in the doorway looking like a picture of spring.

She wore a white eyelet cotton tank top and a lilacsprigged calf-length skirt with a white ruffle at the bottom. Her feet were bare, but her toenails were painted lavender to match her skirt.

"Where did you get that outfit?" he muttered, still feeling foggy and hating the feeling. He decided he'd been out of the game too long.

"You suggested I do some shopping. It's amazing how easy it is once you get in those shops. I found some wonderful things there." She pulled the sides of her skirt out and curtsied. "I decided to wear this right away. The rest are being delivered. I even picked out a few things for you."

Riley rubbed his hand over his face. He was in need of a hot shower, coffee and food. As a sore muscle protected his movement, he added a good massage to the list.

"You look nice." He didn't care if he sounded grudging. He knew he was doing well to sound coherent. He was positive his brain had left him sometime during the night at the same time his body had turned to aches and pains.

"Just nice?" She adjusted the lilac ribbon holding back her hair. "I think I look pretty good, myself. Like a breath of spring," she said the latter as if repeating what someone else had said to her.

"Since it's fall, I guess it's easier to say you look like spring. People don't tend to look like fall, anyway." He rubbed his calf harder as the pain radiated through the muscle. "Damn!"

"Here, let me take care of that." She crouched down in front of him and brushed away his hand. She wrapped her hands around his calf and began kneading the knotted muscles as best she could.

"Hey!" he yelped, trying to pull free of her grip. "That hurts."

"Big baby. It's hurting because it's starting to relax." She tightened her hold and dug her fingers into the muscle. "Don't fight it. It will go easier that way."

He gritted his teeth. "Oh, sure, easy for you to say. You're not the one being tortured by hot needles stuck in your leg."

"There, I can feel the muscle starting to relax." Jenna sat back on her heels. "Why don't you take a hot shower. That should help even more. All that shopping made me hungry and I'm more than ready for some breakfast. The clerk in the dress shop said there are some great hiking trails around here. We can get maps from the concierge."

"I'm in pain and you want to talk about hiking," he grumbled, limping into the bedroom. "We are *not* going hiking."

"I don't know why. It wouldn't hurt. By the way, next time you might think about falling asleep on the couch instead of in a chair," she called after him with laughter in her voice. "That way you won't wake up feeling as if you had been tossed into a cement mixer. Not to mention waking up sounding so cranky."

Riley's response was clearly not meant for mixed company.

"Isn't this gorgeous?" Jenna's voice rang out as she walked ahead of Riley with a steady stride. The path was cleared of pebbles or any holes that might harm a hiker.

She spun around in a circle, her skirt billowing out around her calves. Her white tennis shoes were already colored a light tan from the dust, but she didn't seem to care.

Riley could only stand there and stare at her. He hadn't seen her looking this happy and carefree since before their lives blew up in their faces three years ago. He couldn't imagine how she'd kept it bottled up inside her for so long without exploding. As he studied the sheer joy on her face, he knew why he'd fallen in love with her back then. From the beginning, he couldn't think of anyone else who could express happiness or joy the way Jenna could.

And dammit, if he wasn't careful, he'd fall in love with her all over again.

If he cared to be honest with himself, he'd admit he'd never fallen out of love with her. But then, he never was honest with himself.

Jenna's eyes sparkled with delight as she stopped every so often to examine a small cluster of flowers growing alongside the path.

"The mountain looks so bare, yet these flowers seem to grow right out of the rocks," she exclaimed, touching the delicate petals with her fingertips. "This is the type of scene I would love to sketch and paint with all their colors." Her smile faded as she turned her gaze to her bandage and barely visible fingers.

"Come on, lady, I'm starved," Riley said abruptly, grabbing her other hand and pulling her up. He knew he sounded like a coldhearted SOB, but he also knew Jenna. If she thought too long she would only grow morose. When they said artists could be moody, they were right. Jenna's somber moods were rare, but when they hit, she always preferred to be alone. Since Riley didn't consider himself one of the most cheerful guys around, he hadn't felt rejected by her change in moods and just waited until it passed.

He shifted his backpack that held their lunch. "You said we were hiking up this hill, not stopping to look at every flower along the way," he grumbled good-naturedly.

To his surprise Jenna's mood instantly lightened.

"As long as I'm out in the fresh air, I intend to enjoy every second of it," she told him, slipping her hand out of his and sliding it around his waist. She stumbled when she encountered his gun snugly fitted against the small of his back. She withdrew her hand as if it had been burned.

"We're out in the open, Jenna," he said quietly, easily reading the disquiet on her face. "I'm not about to take any chances."

Her arm fell away. "Sorry, I forgot. You took on this job because they pressured you into it."

He grabbed her wrist and spun her around. "You forgot something else, *sweetheart.* No one, and I mean *no one,* pressures me into anything." His fingers tightened their hold. "The Marshal's Service likes to make sure their charges remain in one piece. You asked for me, and I came. There was no way I was going to let *them* handle the case when I could handle it better," he said without conceit. Just knowledge of what he was capable of.

She tried to pull her arm free, but his hold was firm enough that her efforts were in vain. She knew that when she finally freed herself it was because he allowed it.

"Very well. Then do your job, Marshal, and let's get up this damn hill."

Riley stood there for a moment and watched Jenna, with her head held high, walk ahead of him.

"Damn, she's got a stubborn streak that wasn't there before," he muttered, his gaze warm with admiration.

Jenna had a few choice names to call Riley, but none of them held even a hint of admiration.

Her legs ached from the upward climb, and she was positive a couple of pebbles had found a new home in her shoes. She worried she'd have a blister, but she wasn't about to stop to empty her shoes. Not after her haughty escape from Riley, who she could hear climbing behind her. Muttered curses fell from his lips with each step he took. Since she knew he couldn't see her face, she smiled freely. The pebbles in her shoes and the ache in her legs suddenly didn't feel so bad.

When they reached the top of the hill they found they weren't the only ones to take advantage of the private meadow. Another couple had spread out a blanket and were more engrossed in each other than the beautiful scenery around them.

"I don't think they're dangerous," Jenna said airily. "Can you imagine how much planning would have to be done in hopes we would show up at the same place they were in hopes they could rub us out."

Riley shot her a dark look that easily told her what he thought of her remark. He shrugged off his backpack and dropped it to the ground.

"Did anyone ever tell you that a smart mouth gets you exactly nowhere?"

"Ooh, tough talk from the guy with the badge." She opened the backpack and pulled out the food containers and several bottles of sparkling water.

She looked up and batted her eyes at him, giving him her most guileless expression. "Mr. Macho."

Riley muttered a curse as he dropped to the ground beside her.

"I liked you better the other way," he groused, opening one of the containers and pulling out a chicken breast. He bit into the meat and pulled it free with his teeth.

"The other way. Of course. You're talking about the Jenna who hung on to your every word. The Jenna who agreed with you without reservation. The Jenna who always gazed at you with open admiration like a lost little puppy." She batted her eyes in a flirtatious manner that quickly turned mocking. "Get real, Riley. I was a naive child then. I saw the world as a mass of brilliant colors. A world that I felt was there to entertain me. Give in to my every whim. I didn't look beyond tomorrow because today was too much fun."

She opened another container and spooned seafood salad onto a small plate. She stabbed her fork into the tasty contents then stopped. She looked up. All mockery was gone from her gaze as she stared at him. Now her deep blue eyes were shadowed with sorrow.

"It didn't take me long to learn what it meant to be afraid," she said in a flat voice. "Funny thing,

Riley. I discovered the world isn't as nice as I thought it was. In other words, I grew up.''

In the past his searing gaze would have sent her running because it was so powerful. She wouldn't have known how to handle this side of him. Now she just stared back.

''Sorry, tiger, I think you've lost your touch,'' she mocked.

Riley slowly lowered his gaze until they rested on her breasts. It wasn't long before her nipples tightened against the soft cotton top. His eyes drifted upward, one brow cocked as if to say *I don't think so*.

Jenna calmly poured the sparkling water into two cups and handed one to Riley.

''It may not be icy cold, but it should be sufficient to cool you off.''

Riley's grin was wolfish as he took the cup from her and lifted it in a silent toast.

Jenna was also gracious enough not to gloat. She merely inclined her head in acceptance of his salute.

''Oh, look brownies,'' she murmured, checking another container. ''And I do believe they have cream cheese frosting.'' She dipped her finger into the thick frosting and lifted a bit to her lips. ''Yes, it's definitely cream cheese. Don't expect to get any.'' She protectively cradled the container in her lap.

''You never can tell.''

Considering their conversation during lunch, Jenna was surprised the air wasn't so charged the grass had turned brown.

After they finished eating, Riley helped Jenna clean up and then announced he was taking a nap.

He lay back on the blanket and closed his eyes. It wasn't long before Jenna could hear his snores.

She lay back on the cloth prepared to enjoy the warm, afternoon sun. She knew that while Riley appeared to be deeply asleep, there was still a part of his brain on alert. If anyone came too close to them, he would have been sitting up, looking as if he hadn't just been asleep.

She turned her head slightly, seeing the couple across the meadow. Apparently, they were so engrossed in each other they didn't mind having observers.

Jenna quickly turned away. Partially to give them privacy and partially because watching the lovers brought a warm ache to the center of her body. The only problem was, when she turned away, she was looking at Riley's body.

Closing her eyes didn't erase the sight of the lovers from her brain. There was no doubt lust ran rampant in their veins. And right now, it was starting to run hot in her veins.

She opened her eyes and found Riley lying on his side, his head propped up on his hand. His dark eyes betrayed no emotion, but his body didn't have the ability to hide it.

Jenna said nothing. She just closed her eyes again. It seemed like an eternity before she heard the rustling sounds of Riley's body settling back down.

Jenna was grateful Riley didn't say anything about the charged moment on the mountain during their walk back to the resort. Nor did he say anything when they entered the bungalow.

But she did notice that he went outside to the small pool and swam continuous laps for the next two hours.

When he finally pulled himself out of the water, his chest was heaving and his body shook from the overload. He brushed past her and went into the bathroom. Moments later, the shower was drumming against the tile.

She knew she had a lot to think about. Riley's reason to be with her may have been for protection, but there was more than that between them. They also shared a past. A very intimate past. He told her that was over. After all, she was the one who had ended their relationship.

In retrospect she knew she should have talked it over with him three years ago. She should have insisted to the marshal in charge of her case that she needed to see Riley. She should have sat down with Riley and explained to him why she was entering the Witness Relocation Program. Why she felt she had to enter it alone.

She wondered what she would have done if she'd known then he was planning to leave the Marshal's Service, anyway.

She also wondered what would have happened if she hadn't been in the wrong place at the wrong time. Would she and Riley still have been together? Or would Riley's insistence on no children, and his dark intensity, have pushed her away in the end? Would she have left because she needed more than he could give? So many questions and so few answers she could give herself.

From the beginning, she knew Riley was a

straightforward person. He knew the dark side of life and had even lived it at times. That was his reason for not wanting children. He feared they would end up in that dark side. He hadn't stopped to think that a child of theirs could never be anything but a part of each of them.

Jenna knew little about Riley's life before they were together. It seemed they always had something to talk about other than themselves on a personal level. Now she wished they had talked more about themselves.

She scanned her memory. She knew he had no family. At least, he'd never mentioned any to her. She hadn't met too many of his friends, and he'd pretty much kept her away from people he worked with. His apartment was so sterile, it could even have passed for a motel room. That was why he'd moved into her loft.

She stifled a soft sigh of regret. She missed her loft with all its windows and a postcard view of the beach.

It had been the first time she'd lived on her own, so she'd allowed her creativity to blossom. Window treatments had been bold primary colors while cream-painted walls were covered with her paintings. Other walls were painted in equally bold colors to denote the different rooms.

When Riley moved in with her, his idea of decorating was to bring his clothing in a couple of suitcases and a lockbox for his weapons.

That was something else she learned: law enforcement didn't refer to them as guns but weapons. And law enforcement officers didn't always have glamorous jobs where they worked undercover, driving around in fancy cars and hobnobbing with the upper echelon of criminals.

She knew little about Riley's work. He had kept quiet about it, and she knew better than to ask. Instead she tried not to worry, the nights he wasn't there. She never told him of the fear she experienced when he was gone without a word for days on end. She refused to watch any television program that featured police work of any kind. She never wanted to think he could be hurt and bleeding somewhere. Or worse.

In the past few days she'd come to know more about his work than she had before. And what she saw, she freely admitted she didn't like.

Even during dinner nothing was said about the tension that radiated between them that afternoon.

Jenna was startled when she saw the couple she'd seen earlier. They may have been sitting across from each other in a formal dining room, but the expressions on their faces said they would have preferred a great deal more privacy.

"I know they like to recommend all the fresh fish here, but I'd still rather have a good steak," Riley muttered, glancing at the menu.

"You might want to remember fish is healthier for you," Jenna murmured, already deciding on scallops.

"Good. Because I'm still having a steak."

"You had steak last night. Why can't you try something else?"

"Last night I had New York cut. Tonight, I'll have filet mignon. How's that?"

"No difference in my mind."

Jenna tried to be discreet, but she couldn't help feeling curious about their fellow diners. A few faces were familiar, but there were also some new ones. Some sported painful-looking sunburns as they shifted uncomfortably in their chairs.

"It looks as if more than a few guests should have considered sunblock today." She picked up a soft breadstick and bit into it. She smiled as the taste of garlic and butter exploded in her mouth.

Riley winced as he glanced at the sunburn victims.

"I guess they were thinking more about getting a tan than the effects of too many hours under the sun," he said in a low voice. "How long do you think it will take before they start peeling?"

She wrinkled her nose. "I don't want to think about it. I couldn't believe I burned so badly when we were at Lake Havasu. The burn was bad enough, but the peeling was worse. I looked like a patchwork quilt for days."

"You did look pretty funny." He grinned as he snatched the last breadstick out of the basket.

"I'm so glad you thought it was hilarious," she said sarcastically. "You get a sunburn and peel. Let's see how you feel when you're itching all the time."

Riley's eyes suddenly darkened as if a delicious memory came to mind.

Then Jenna's memory took an abrupt turn as she remembered the nights she'd itched so badly. And how Riley had soothed her fevered skin with a silky lotion that smelled of vanilla and honey.

He had warmed it between his hands before he slowly applied to her skin. He had taken his time, making sure he hadn't left one inch untouched. She had treasured that memory for many a long night when she felt so alone.

She picked up her wineglass and gulped down half the contents.

A hand reached out and grabbed hold of her wrist before she drank more.

"Be careful, Smitty. That stuff's pretty potent. Why not try the water instead?"

"I picked up the wrong glass," she lied, setting the wineglass back on the table. To further her lie, she picked up her water glass and drank deeply.

"Well, as I live and breathe. Hey there, old buddy!" A Texas twang warned them before a man's hand clapped Riley's back. "What the hell you doing down here, son?"

Riley looked up at the man towering over him. "Same as you, Seth. Picking up some sun." He glanced behind the man and gave a questioning glance. A statuesque brunette squeezed into a leather tank style dress stood there looking bored.

"This here's my wife, Mitzi," Seth explained. He glanced over at Jenna. "I don't believe I've met this lady."

"Jennifer," Riley said crisply. "My wife."

Seth grinned broadly. "Well, hell, son, I never thought you'd get yourself hooked. Not after all those nights we hung out together. But then, I guess that's why you'd be here since it is a honeymoon resort."

Riley turned to Jenna as he spoke, "Let's just say she's very special." He turned back to Seth. "What about you?"

He shrugged. "Mitzi used to work in one of my clubs. She wanted to go to Paris, but I told her I wasn't going all the way over there for what I can get here."

"Seth," Mitzi turned his name into three syllables with a pure Brooklyn accent. "Are we gonna eat or what?"

"Or what, baby," he leered. He waved his hand at her. "All right. All right." He leaned over to Riley. "I gotta tell you she's the one. It took me four times, but I know this marriage will last." He looked at Jenna. "Nice to meet you." He walked off with a swagger that appeared to go with his over-the-top personality.

Jenna picked at her salad. "Don't tell me. His clubs cater to those lonely businessmen from out of town. And he employs ladies, and I use that word loosely, who are more than willing to keep them company for an exorbitant fee. I gather his wife recently retired from the business." She chose a cherry tomato and brought it to her lips.

"That's Seth, all right," Riley agreed, working on his salad. "You know, each time he's gotten married, he's said the same thing about his wife. This one probably won't last any longer than the others."

"I do declare, you meet some of the most interesting people," she drawled.

Riley grinned and shook his head.

"I'm not so sure I can handle all these changes in you, Smitty."

"Tough. Live with it. The new me is doing just fine."

Chapter 8

The muted sound of water splashing wouldn't have been enough to wake up most people. But then, Riley wasn't most people.

When he glanced in the bedroom, he didn't expect to find an indentation in the mattress and an empty pillow. Had he slept so soundly he hadn't even heard her leave the room?

"Some damn fine protection you are, Cooper," he muttered. "You should have gone with your first instinct and stayed in here with her at night. That's what you get for being a nice guy."

He noticed the French doors he'd closed and locked last thing now stood open. He walked over and looked outside. While he stood there, he saw a sight that literally took his breath away.

Jenna swam back and forth with the grace of a seal, with only the moonlight for covering.

At each end of the small pool, she surfaced long enough to draw in a gulp of air and dove back under to glide through the water back to the other side.

Riley couldn't move as he stood there and watched the otherworldly sight that sent a white-hot fire streaking through his belly.

He remembered the many late nights when they would wander across a deserted stretch of beach. And he would urge her to swim nude. Every time she refused for fear someone would come upon them.

Until one hot summer night when they'd taken a long drive up the coast. At one point they got out and walked and stumbled onto a secluded cove. Jenna shed her clothing, ran into the water and then screamed how cold it was. Soon the cold hadn't mattered when Riley had warmed her with his body.

He remained standing in the doorway, content to watch her swim. At least he knew she was safe.

But not safe from him.

Riley had no idea how long he stood there watching her swim. She still had no idea he was standing there.

It was some minutes later when she climbed out. She snatched up a towel that lay on the cement by the pool. She wrapped it around her body, then lifted her arms to slick back her hair. With the moonlight streaming down on her body, she looked like a silvery wraith.

She slowly turned until she faced the bungalow. She didn't say a word as she stood there looking at his shadowed figure standing in the doorway. Words weren't necessary.

Riley stepped out of the darkness of the room and

walked toward her. When he stood in front of her, he grasped her by the waist and lifted her onto the low stone wall. The towel parted and dropped down to pool around her hips, but neither of them noticed. Or cared.

He still didn't speak as he ran his hands along the sides of her head, feeling the cool moisture against his palms. He kept his hands flat against her hair.

When she lifted her face, her lips were slightly parted. A droplet of water still shimmering on her lower lip caught his attention. He lowered his head, his tongue catching that droplet and taking it back into his mouth. His mouth returned to hers in a kiss designed to steal her breath away as it cajoled, tempted and seduced.

He didn't touch her any other place than his mouth on hers and his hands framing her face. She didn't refuse him nor did she move away. She sat there allowing him to refamiliarize himself with her taste.

Words weren't necessary when actions spoke louder.

Jenna soon raised her arms and looped them around Riley's neck. Her movement caused her body to arch up and press closer to his. He carefully grasped her injured wrist as if to examine the damp bandages. He nuzzled her palm and pressed a kiss against the center of her palm.

The heat of his body dried her damp skin as he bent his head to nibble the sensitive skin along the curve of her neck. She closed her eyes, slightly bending her neck to one side in a silent invitation.

The only sounds heard were the ragged sounds of their breathing, muted sounds of insects and even fainter sounds of music and laughter coming from the resort. They weren't alone except in their minds. They knew each other so well that each touch was guaranteed heaven. They knew each other's weak points and where pleasure was the greatest. They were intent on giving each other pleasure.

Jenna's parted lips slid along Riley's jawline down to his throat. She delicately sank her teeth into the slightly rough skin to taste the tangy salt of his flesh.

Riley felt the hunger rise up in him with white-hot urgency. Her scent was an aphrodisiac he hadn't experienced in some time, but his memory was infallible. The faint chlorine scent of her skin didn't detract from her personal scent. A scent that he could have identified if he stood blindfolded in a room with a hundred other women surrounding him.

No other woman ever slaked his hunger the way Jenna did. He moved his head, returning to her mouth to plunder its inner sweetness. His tongue plunged downward, mimicking the loveplay they had once indulged in so lightheartedly and so intensely. The loveplay his body ached to recreate. Except he instinctively knew their joining wouldn't be the light-hearted play they participated in before. There was too much between them. For now, hunger was the strongest emotion.

He wouldn't have it any other way.

He burned when he felt her hands running across his chest. When her fingertips found his nipples and circled the hard nubs, he felt ready to explode.

His hold on her face tightened but was still so gentle her skin would not be marked by his possessive touch.

His kiss deepened, sweeping her into a world of fiery mystery that sent her soaring. She wound her legs around his waist, arching up against his arousal. With no clothing between them, there was no way he could hide it. Not with Jenna rubbing against him and whimpering low in her throat. With her legs wrapped tightly around him, they were as close as they could be.

When she reached down and circled his hardness with her hand to guide him into her, there was no stopping either of them. He thrust into her, feeling as if he'd finally come home. Riley wasn't sure whether he cursed or prayed as he felt Jenna draw him inside. Her tight velvety walls sheathed him and pulled him in even farther.

Riley could feel his neck muscles tighten to the point of pain as he remained still, hoping to regain his control. He had to close his eyes to better savor the joy he hadn't experienced in such a long time.

The soft sounds from Jenna's lips seemed to dance across his skin at the same time as her lips stroked his flesh.

He withdrew slowly even as agony ripped through him. And then paused before thrusting inside again. His strokes were slow and steady, determined as he was to make this last as long as possible.

Jenna's nails dug into his shoulders, and he felt her muscles start to tighten around him. Experience told him that as long as he kept their loving slow it would only build up the tension between them until they were both quivering with sensual pain that enhanced their pleasure to the extreme. Her soft whimpers built in intensity as his own body tightened to the explosion point.

When Jenna opened her mouth to scream, Riley's mouth covered hers with a deep probing kiss. She could only cling to him as they raced to the stars.

This was nothing like the many times they had made love before. This was a passion that had built up over the years apart, and it could only be quenched by their union. Quenched then reborn.

By the time Riley shot his release into Jenna, she was a pulsing mass of exposed nerves. She felt as if he would only have to run his fingertips across the surface of her skin and she would explode again.

She kept her legs wrapped around his waist because she didn't have the strength to release them. Her hands remained locked on his shoulders, and she rested her cheek against his chest. His skin was damp, and under her ear she could hear the heavy thud that she was sure echoed her own racing heartbeat. She wasn't sure she could utter one word.

She could feel Riley's lips moving against her temple.

"Do you think we sent the Richter scale into infinity?" he asked in a low voice.

Jenna took a couple of deep breaths to steady her pulse.

"Massive earthquake in Mexico sent an exclusive resort sliding into the sea. Film at eleven," she said finally.

He chuckled. "That good, huh, Smitty?"

"You knew it was, so don't go looking for compliments, Cooper."

He kept his arms around her. "Hold on." He kept

her wrapped around him as he walked to the pool and descended the steps into the water. When they were waist-deep, Jenna let go and floated away. Her arms moved lazily through the water as she watched him with a gaze that told him nothing.

"If you're looking for an apology, you've come to the wrong place," he told her.

"I don't recall acting like the wounded virgin." She flopped back and floated. "The tension had been building up between us from the beginning. After all, we'd been lovers at one time. It was a natural conclusion we'd have sex sooner or later."

"Natural conclusion?" he repeated. *"Sex?"* He made his way closer to her. "Smitty, what we just had was more than sex. It was way out there in the cosmos. It was better than good."

Jenna continued treading water as she listened to Riley's tirade. He may have kept his voice soft so no one could overhear, but it was no less intense.

She didn't want him to know how much it meant to her, but she didn't think he would believe she meant what she said about it being just sex. All she knew was that making love with him was even more soul shattering than it had been before. She had no idea how long they would have together, and she didn't want him to think she saw more in their love-making than might have been there.

"Yes, but no matter how good what we just had was, it doesn't mean we won't have a parting of ways when your assignment is over," she told him before she swam past him in the direction of the steps. She climbed out and retrieved her towel from the wall. She acted as if what they just had was an everyday occurrence.

It wasn't so dark that Riley couldn't see how badly her hands trembled as she dried herself off. Or the stark expression in her eyes just before she looked away from him.

Riley allowed her to get as far as the door before he caught up with her. Fury was etched on his face, but his touch was gentle.

"Sorry, sweetheart, but you always were a lousy liar," he muttered, gathering her up in his arms and fastening his mouth on hers.

If he expected an argument, it wasn't forthcoming. As he laid her on the tumbled covers, Jenna's arms lifted to pull him down beside her. Her eagerness electrified him as it had done before.

And as before, there were no words spoken, because their bodies seemed to do a better job than their mouths ever could.

Riley woke up feeling better than he had in a long time. He kept his eyes closed as he felt the energy race through his body. He knew he was grinning from ear to ear. Something he hadn't done a lot of lately. But then, an event like last night hadn't been in his life for a long time, either. Something along the lines of three years.

"Why don't you just get up and beat your chest with your fists and howl at the sun?" An amused voice interrupted his internal joy. "It's no secret that's what you really want to do."

He opened his eyes. Jenna was dressed in red cotton shorts and a red-and-white-print tank top that barely skimmed the shorts' waistband. When she moved the fabric shifted just enough to reveal a strip of lightly tanned skin.

After they'd come back inside, they'd rewrapped her hand with an elastic bandage that shone a bright pink against her arm.

"Couldn't you find anything to match your jewelry?" he asked, nodding toward her arm.

She held her arm up, striking a model's pose. "I thought this would make a nice contrast."

Riley breathed a silent sigh of relief. Jenna's manner told him she had no regrets about the previous night.

He knew he didn't have any. If anything, he regretted there would come a time he would have to give her up again.

By rights, he shouldn't have made love to her. He should have continued with the cold showers and kept her at arm's length. He also recalled they both hadn't thought of protection. Riley only hoped it was a safe time for her.

He should have remembered he'd taken her on as an assignment. He'd deliberately tagged her in his mind as an assignment so he wouldn't consider any personal feelings.

He should have known better.

Jenna leaned against the dresser with her arms crossed in front of her chest.

Riley noticed with great interest her action plumped her breasts up above her arms.

"I thought about heading over to the lanai for breakfast, but I knew you wouldn't have been happy with me for going without you. Therefore, I am starving and impatiently waiting for you to get your tired old body out of bed and into the shower.'' She arched an eyebrow.

Riley winced at her challenge. He was out of bed in a flash and on his way to the bathroom. Before he reached it, he stopped in front of Jenna. He crooked his arm around her neck and brought her to him for a hard and very thorough kiss.

"Not all *that* old, and not all that tired," he murmured, when he released her.

Uncaring he was naked, he went into the bathroom. Jenna barely had time to take a deep breath before she heard the drumming of the shower. She delicately ran her tongue across her lower lip. She imagined she could still taste him.

"No, definitely not old and tired."

When Jenna and Riley entered the lanai dining area, Sasha greeted them in his courtly manner and suggested they join them.

"My grandson is by the swimming pool with his nanny watching over him. He seems to prefer swimming to eating breakfast, although he will later complain he is very hungry and ask why I didn't feed him," he explained, then he gestured to the waiter to fill Jenna's and Riley's coffee cups. "I would appreciate the company." He turned to Jenna. "Are you enjoying your visit?"

"I find it relaxing," she murmured, smiling her thanks to the busboy as he filled her waterglass. "It's amazing how much there is to do around here."

"Yes, there are some fascinating tours offered to some of the Indian burial grounds and ancient temples," Sasha told her. "You should insist your husband take you on one of them."

"I'll have to think about that." She pushed back her chair. "If you gentlemen will excuse me, I am taking advantage of the buffet. I love the idea of eating as much as I'd like," she said with a mischievous smile.

Sasha watched her walk away. He had on his face the smile of a man enjoying a lovely sight. He turned back to Riley, his smile disappearing as quickly as it had appeared.

"You are not what you appear to be, my friend," he said.

Riley sipped his coffee before replying. "Oh? What am I supposed to be?"

"A man and his wife on their honeymoon, like so many others here." The older man waved his hand to encompass the others seated at nearby tables.

"Funny, that's what I thought I was doing," Riley said easily.

"I have lived a long time, Ryan. And during that time, I have met many men. Not all of them lived on the right side of the law. There is something about you that does not make me think of a young husband enjoying the nights with his wife."

Riley felt the weight of his weapon nestled against his back. A not-so-subtle reminder why he was there.

He knew Sasha was an old man, but there was no doubt he wasn't feeble in mind or body. His hands were steady as they held the coffee cup and his eyes clear. He might not know the story, but he did sense Riley and Jenna weren't exactly who they said they were.

Now all Riley had to figure out was why Sasha cared about their identity. He wasn't worried about himself. He worried what would happen to Jenna.

Sasha hadn't missed Riley's quick sideways glance toward Jenna.

"If I felt the two of you were hiding from the authorities I would have done something about it. But I have a feeling you are here because Jennifer is the one in trouble. And not because she has done something wrong."

Riley noticed Jenna carrying a loaded plate and walking back to the table. He only had a few seconds to say what he felt he could to the older man.

"There's someone out there who's as filthy as they come. He wants her dead because she spoke the truth three years ago," he muttered before she came too close. "He got a little too close once, and I'm making sure it doesn't happen again."

Sasha immediately and smoothly steered the conversation elsewhere.

It wasn't until later, when Jenna returned to the buffet table, that he turned back to Riley.

"Someone tried to hurt her," he said, with a slight frown.

"That someone did hurt her, and I have an idea he wants to kill her," Riley said flatly. "A man she testified against three years ago set this up."

Sasha shook his head. "I see what you mean. She is a protected witness someone wants gone." The older man looked pained. "An innocent caught up in another's web. Why did you bring her here?"

Riley smiled wryly. "I didn't have a lot of time

when it came to travel plans. This seemed like a good idea."

Sasha smiled back. "Do your superiors know the two of you have become lovers?"

Riley shifted uncomfortably under the man's shrewd gaze.

"We were together some time ago, before her life blew up in her face," he admitted.

"So you protect her because of a shared past." He nodded his understanding. "Do not worry. I will not give away your secret. I am made aware of all our new guests. I cannot imagine that type of man would find you here, but you cannot be too careful, can you?"

He was surprised by the man's more-than-generous offer. And a little suspicious. "Pardon me for being blunt, but why are you willing to help us? I could have spun a pretty incredible story."

"I've lived too many years to know whether a man is lying or not. You are not. I left Russia and came here to give my family a better life. Jennifer reminds me of my daughter. She looks as delicate as a flower, but inside she is tempered steel. The two of you complement each other."

Riley chuckled. "I don't know if I'd tell her that. But I have to say, if I'm going to hide out it may as well be somewhere as comfortable as here."

Sasha smiled back. "Then we will do all we can to make your stay all you wish it to be."

Sasha leaned back as the waiter refilled his coffee cup. "I like your Jennifer. She is a lovely woman. As long as she is on the hotel grounds, you need not worry about her safety."

Riley sat there, for the first time unsure what to say. He knew he'd taken a chance, confiding in Sasha, but he felt he'd done the right thing.

"How do you expect to eat all of that food after the first plate you polished clean?" Sasha teased Jenna as she sat down.

She smiled at Riley, then turned to Sasha. "There was no way I'd pass up all this wonderful fresh fruit." She picked up a strawberry and held it out to Riley, who obediently opened his mouth for her.

"She has you well trained, Ryan," Sasha joked. "She appears to have you eating out of her hand."

"When she offers strawberries like that one, I'll definitely bite." He grinned.

"Then we will keep you well supplied with strawberries," Sasha promised Jenna.

Riley was still realizing what just happened between the two men. A one-sided bargain in Riley's favor.

No matter what, no one would be allowed to harm Jenna as long as they stayed here.

"They're in Mexico," he announced to his employer, feeling tremendous relief he had succeeded instead of failed. He feared he would not have been given much more time before the other man grew impatient and replaced him with someone else.

The man's eyes were the color of cold steel. "Are you positive?"

He nodded and went on to explain how he'd been able to find out where Jenna and Riley were staying. Now that he had given his employer the good news, he realized he was going to have to dispense the bad news.

"Getting to them could be difficult," he said hesitantly. "It's a resort that caters to couples. Honeymooners and couples celebrating special anniversaries."

The employer's smile would have frightened a shark. "Nothing is difficult if you have enough money to pay the right people. And I have more than enough money. I want them taken care of by the end of the week." He lit his cigar and turned away.

The man was effectively dismissed.

He walked out of the office and headed for the elevator.

He'd heard the orders and hadn't liked them. He was just told to go to Mexico. He never did like the country. He didn't speak the language, didn't really have all that many contacts down there, and the last time he was there he'd suffered constant heartburn from the food and there were times he feared even the bottled water was impure.

He enjoyed his work with the glee of a sadist. But there was a sadist even better than him. His employer was the one who had perfected the art. That was why he enjoyed taking his employer's money—as long as he didn't have to face his employer too often. The man scared the hell out of him. And very little scared him.

Sometimes he wondered if death wouldn't be a better alternative.

Chapter 9

As the days passed, Jenna felt a shift in the air. She sensed the change as surely as if something tangible brushed past her and left its imprint on her skin.

It didn't take her long to figure out when she first felt it. She could trace it back to the day she and Riley had shared breakfast with Sasha.

While she had been picking and choosing at the buffet table, she now sensed the two men had come to some unspoken agreement. An unspoken agreement that had to do with her.

She told herself she shouldn't have any complaints. By now they had been here for close to ten days. If it hadn't been for the mornings, when Riley insisted on teaching her his own brand of self-defense, she would have thought they were there for a leisurely vacation.

She played the role of a sloth on the afternoons

she and Riley spent on the beach, or enjoyed the times they made use of the hiking trails. She especially enjoyed the dinners she and Riley had shared with Sasha and his grandson on more than one evening.

With Riley's assistance and Sasha's amused supervision, Jenna and the little boy spent one morning building an elaborate sand castle complete with a moat and a dragon standing guard.

"I'd say that's one fine castle, little Sasha," Riley commented, walking up to them.

Jenna and little Sasha stood back to admire their handiwork.

"But the dragon cannot breathe fire!" the little boy mourned as he sat back down on the sand. "Dragons are supposed to breathe fire to scare away the bad men."

"Perhaps it is just as well your dragon doesn't breathe fire," Sasha said to console his grandson as he joined them. "It is too hot a day for a fire."

Jenna pulled the boy to her and hugged him. "Our dragon doesn't need to breathe fire. People will be scared of him just because he looks so fierce."

He didn't look convinced by their words, but he soon perked up and ran for the water's edge with his frazzled-looking nanny close on his heels.

"Luckily he swims like a fish." Sasha chuckled as the adult trio walked back to a row of lounge chairs. "Children are special, but grandchildren are created from the heart," he added.

Riley immediately stretched out on a sand lounge. His eyes were covered with his sunglasses, and his dark tanned skin glistened with sweat.

"Especially when the parents take off for another honeymoon and Grandpa takes over," he teased. "You can spoil him to your heart's content then hand him back to Mom and Dad who get to calm him down after all this fun."

"That is what grandparents are for," Sasha reminded him. "What I hope is that they will think of having another child. Sasha should not be an only child."

"But he's obviously loved, and that's what counts," Jenna pointed out. For a moment her smile faltered, and the expression in her eyes as she watched the energetic little boy could only be described as wistful.

Sasha beamed with pride. "He will be a great man when he grows up. I will see to that."

Riley grinned. "Then keep him out of politics."

Jenna groaned as she felt the shift in the conversation. "No discussion on world politics, please?" She covered her face. "Once you start you can't stop. And the two of you never agree!"

"That is why we enjoy our discussions." Sasha fingered a nonfiction book written about World War II battles in Europe.

Jenna flopped back on her towel and covered her face with her hat. She thought about applying another layer of sunblock, but she felt too lazy to move.

"At least your 'discussions' as you call them are a great reason for me to take a nap," she mumbled.

The last thing she heard as she drifted off into a light sleep was the men chuckling before they dove into their spirited conversation.

Jenna felt herself float in a soft netherworld of sleep with Riley always present.

How could a man who displayed the patience of a saint while entertaining a little boy not want children of his own?

It was a question she knew would always haunt her because she wouldn't have an answer.

Her sleep-filled brain started to drift in another direction as she recalled their lovemaking.

That night they'd made love by the pool turned out to be just the beginning. Each night after that they shared a bed and shared their bodies. And each time Riley never forgot protection.

It had gotten to where Jenna believed she couldn't sleep unless Riley's body was curved spoon fashion around her. Sometimes she felt as if the past three years had been nothing more than a bad dream.

She asked herself if the idea of their returning to their old habits as if nothing had happened was a good idea.

Could she tempt fate by thinking of them having a future together? For all she knew, when this was all over, she would be returned to the Witness Relocation Program again and Riley would return to whatever he was doing. And even if he didn't, she couldn't think of their having a future together. All she knew was that they would have to sit down and have a long talk when things settled down.

She wasn't the same person she'd been three years ago, and Riley wasn't the same, either. Could they work past whatever differences they might have now and forge something new and even stronger?

All she could do was tell herself that as long as something wasn't spoken out loud, it didn't exist.

She awoke to find Riley towering over her. "You know, a nap sounds like a good idea," he said casually.

"I'm sure it's necessary for boys," Jenna said in an equally casual tone. "Probably even more necessary for old men."

"Old man?" he scoffed. "I'll show you old man."

Jenna squealed as Riley picked her up and tossed her over his shoulder.

She was still screaming his name and cursing him as he stood waist-deep in the water with her now held high in his arms.

"Are you absolutely sure you don't want to take back what you just called me?" he asked. The devilish twinkle in his eyes told her either way she wasn't safe.

She lifted her chin. "I suggest you take me back to dry land before you regret your actions," she said haughtily.

Riley pretended to drop her and laughed at her shriek of outrage.

"Stop it!" she screamed.

"Okay." He opened his arms and she promptly fell in the water.

Jenna shot upward, sputtering and coughing. She hissed a curse at the same time she dove at his knees, easily knocking him off balance. Riley fell backward, completely submerged. Jenna laughed and began a victory dance at besting her opponent. Then she noticed he hadn't come back up.

"Riley?" she said tentatively, looking for a sign as she splashed the water with her hands. "This isn't funny, Riley. Riley!" She started sounding frantic as he still hadn't appeared.

She barely had time to draw a breath of air as her ankles were grabbed and she was pulled under the water and into Riley's arms. His kiss was designed to draw that very air out of her and into him. She relaxed and looped her arms around his neck as he easily slid them into deeper water.

Jenna could feel Riley's hardness seeking her out as she lay flat against him. They were both breathless as they floated to the surface. She was surprised to see how far out from the shore they'd gone.

Riley loosened his hold, and she rolled over to float on her back. Their fingertips touched as they allowed the gentle waves to move them in a slow circle.

Jenna looked up at the sky and exhaled a deep sigh.

"What was that for?" Riley asked.

"It's just so beautiful," she replied. She pulled her fingers from his loose grasp and allowed them to drift down to the hem of his trunks. "Think it's possible without drowning?" she asked.

Riley cocked an eyebrow. "Why, Miss Welles, I am well and truly shocked."

"Since we're out in deeper water than the pool, I thought I'd at least ask." she grinned. "Come on, Cooper. Where's that adventurous spirit of yours?"

"I may believe in being prepared, but I don't always think about it if we're planning to take a swim," he told her.

"From what I could see, this swim wasn't planned." She passed her fingers across his trunks. "Not to mention, in case you've forgotten, I am on the pill."

Riley swam away from her.

Puzzled by his action, Jenna looked after him.

"What's wrong?" she called after him.

"I don't have to spell it out for you, Jen. Come on, we better swim back in." He swam toward the shore with strong powerful strokes.

Jenna swam back at a slower pace. By the time she reached the beach, Riley was already crossing the sand to the two chairs that held their towels.

"I should have realized you weren't going to touch me unless you had protection with you," she said in a low voice, as she picked up her towel and dried off her shoulders and arms. She used her fingers to comb back her hair and squeeze the excess water out.

He didn't look at her as he dried himself off. "We got a scare that first time. We can't afford for anything to happen."

"Of course not," she murmured, picking up her sunglasses and slipping them on. She felt she needed them and not just to block out the glare.

Riley shot her a narrowed look. "Of course not," he mocked. "The pill isn't infallible, Jen. We know that now."

She refused to flinch under his accusing tone. "Or maybe your sperm think they're just too macho to let a pill deter them." She picked up her towel, sunblock and book. "Don't worry about going to the bungalow with me. With the mood I'm in right now, I doubt anyone would dare bother me."

Riley watched her walk away with her back straight and head held high.

"Oh yeah, no man in his right mind would take you on," he muttered. "But then, I've never been in my right mind around you."

He was positive he was going to die. The bottled water turned out not to be so safe after all. Not to mention the small towns he had to drive through didn't offer much in accommodations or restaurants.

His stomach rumbled unpleasantly. Even antacids couldn't settle it.

The Jeep he rented didn't have power steering and had to have been built during World War II. Every bone in his body ached from the rocky roads he had been forced to take to reach his destination.

Even now he wasn't close to where he needed to be.

He was lucky, though. He'd found a man who worked at the hotel as a bellman and the man had many children to feed. A little extra money came in handy, and the bellman was willing to tell the *gringo* whatever he needed to know.

He vowed that after this assignment was over, he was taking a nice long vacation where the water was sanitized, the food edible and the beds didn't have bugs in them.

With the woman dead, he'd have more than enough money to go wherever he wanted.

And far away from the man who'd made his life a complete hell.

A variety of multicolored brochures landed not so neatly in Riley's lap. He looked up at Jenna, who stood over him.

"Thank you for the reading material, but I have enough right here." He held up the book he had been reading.

"There are guided tours available for the guests," she reminded him. "Since we've been here, there hasn't been a hint that anyone has found us, has there?" She didn't bother to wait for a reply. "So why can't we take one of the tours?"

Riley stuck his finger between the pages to hold his place as he used his free hand to pick up a brochure and study it.

"We'd be in a group. All perfectly safe," she recited. "You know, 'safety in numbers' and all that. There should be no reason why we can't go."

"You're safe here." He dropped the brochure on the table and returned to his book.

Jenna snatched the book out of his hands and dropped it on the floor. She swung her leg around and planted herself in his lap.

"Do you know what I have done in the past week?"

He considered her demand for a moment. "Let's see. You rediscovered windsurfing and how bad you've always been at it. You've built two mega sand castles. You spent one day at the spa with all those wraps and a massage and facials and whatever else they do to you in there. All in all, I'd say you've had a fun time."

"And now I want to go someplace where there isn't a beach or a spa or a swimming pool," she stated. "I want to take the tour that goes to the temples."

"If you look in the gift shop you'll find postcards showing the temples from every side." He tried to lean down to retrieve his book, but she blocked his every attempt. "Don't even think about mailing any of them out to friends, though. This isn't a vacation, you know."

"It isn't? You've sure done your part to make it seem like one. Have you talked to Dave?"

He looked surprised by her sudden switch in subject. "Just this morning. He sends his regards."

"And did he have anything new to report?"

He heaved a deep sigh. "No, but that doesn't mean anything. We think they're keeping their activities as quiet as possible. But there have been some inquiries made about you. He's running down the rumors."

"But no one has shown up here," Jenna said. "Besides, my looks have changed. Even more so."

"True." Riley's gaze wandered over her barely clad body with more than a hint of interest.

Jenna had been sunbathing on the patio and wore a bronze-colored bikini that highlighted the deep tan she had acquired during her stay. Her hair had lightened even more from her days in the sun, and pampering from the hotel spa had left her skin looking luminous. She smelled of coconut-scented lotion and her own personal scent.

He wondered if he could get away with loosening the string holding her bikini top intact. Even though no one could see them when they relaxed on their patio, she refused to sunbathe topless.

"Haven't you read all the reports written about the sun and skin cancer?" he asked her in an amiable voice.

"I wear sunblock. Don't change the subject, Riley. I want to take that tour," she said stubbornly.

Her unconscious shifting in his lap wasn't helping his concentration any. He finally grabbed hold of her by the waist to keep her still.

"Not a good idea, Smitty." He kept his gaze level with hers, but her eyes remained fixed on his.

Riley had to admire Jenna for her persistence. He didn't know when she'd gotten this stubborn streak. He didn't remember her having it before. Right now he was privately cursing her for having one, but he still had to admire her.

"I'll check it out," he said finally.

She had the grace not to show her triumph.

"Day after tomorrow."

"You have to sign up for it in advance."

Riley shot her a level look. "Trust me, Jen. You won't have a problem getting on the tour of your choice." He reached around her and this time successfully snagged his book.

Jenna climbed off his lap and backed up to sit on the small table by Riley's chair. "When are we returning to the States?"

"If Dave hears what he wants to hear, we should be able to go back in the next week or so."

Jenna ran her fingers lightly across her bandaged

hand. Discomfort was at a minimum now. The doctor had examined and X-rayed it the day before and announced it was healing nicely.

She moved her fingers as little as possible, even though the pain was almost nonexistent. The bruising was gone and the skin was a healthy pink, but she had no idea if she still had dexterity.

She spent an hour each day practicing writing her name with her left hand. Her name finally looked legible, but she hadn't tried writing anything else much less attempting to draw. She was too afraid of failure.

Riley noticed Jenna's absent air and easily gauged the direction of her thoughts. He didn't need to see her touching her hand to understand what was bothering her.

"I wouldn't worry about it, Jen."

She looked up. "Worry about what?"

"What you worried about before. Playing the violin. You never could before, and you're tone-deaf to boot."

Jenna rolled her eyes. "Not funny, Cooper."

He leaned over and covered her wrist with his hand. "It was a vicious attack. One meant to cripple you. In mind and body," he said quietly. "Especially the mind. You can't let them win, Smitty. You're a strong woman, and you'll come out fine."

She remained so still for a moment he wondered if she even heard him.

"You still think someone will come for me, don't you?" Her low-voiced question hung in the air like an executioner's ax.

"They won't stop looking." He didn't coat the truth, because he didn't want her too relaxed.

The light in Jenna's eyes died. She rose to her feet and walked back inside.

Riley muttered a pithy curse. He knew he had given her too much freedom in the past week. He kept a close eye on her, but she still roamed around the resort.

Even though Sasha assured him she was safe, Riley still couldn't dismiss the feeling that they were living in the eye of a hurricane. He knew he couldn't go to the man for any further assistance.

What Sasha provided he did of his own free will for Jenna's sake. Riley also knew that being in the older man's debt wasn't a good idea. Those kind of debts were expected to be repaid.

Things had been going too well for way too long. If it wasn't that he knew exactly why they were there, he could make himself believe he and Jenna were back together again and they were down here for a vacation.

He shouldn't have kept her here for as long as he had. They should have been on the move before now, but he wasn't sure where they would go if they had to leave here. He had hoped it would be cleared up before now. His calls to Dave hadn't been fruitful. If anything, they were frustrating, because Dave hadn't been able to find out anything.

He had kept his calls short so they couldn't be traced.

Riley looked down at his book. The fast-paced psychological thriller couldn't hold his attention now. He even wondered why he started reading it in the first place. Real life tended to have more conspiracies than any book could hold. He set the book aside and went out to find her.

"You mean we can go on one of the tours?" Jenna looked at him as if afraid he might suddenly change his mind.

He inwardly winced that she was so suspicious of him. Even though he knew exactly why. "I guess I haven't made your life all that easy these past few years," he said slowly as he pulled a pale green T-shirt over his head.

Jenna turned away and bent closer to peer into the mirror as she applied lipstick.

"I told you before. I made the choice. Everything was fully explained to me. I was an adult, Riley. No one forced me into it."

"Yeah, and I know all about those explanations." He walked over and slid his arms around her waist, pulling her back against him. "Wouldn't you rather stay here?" he murmured, nuzzling the soft hollow of her throat. The warm floral fragrance of her skin was starting to give him ideas. "We could play doctor and insatiable nurse," he said, tongue firmly in cheek. "You check my temperature. I check yours. We see whose is higher."

She shook her head at him, smiling as if he was an incorrigible small child.

"Act your age. We cannot miss seeing temples that have been in existence for thousands of years." She briefly leaned against him. "This is a chance to experience history. We can go out there and act like typical tourists. I'll take your picture standing in front of one of the temples, and you can take mine.''

"Just as long as no one else gets in the photos we'd be fine.'' He groaned and stood back. "All right, but this is still against my better judgment.''

Jenna looped her arms around his neck and lightly bumped her forehead against his chin in a teasing gesture. "Riley, I'll be careful. I won't go off by myself and I'll always remain in sight. I just wanted to do something different.''

"Damn straight you will stay close to me,'' he growled.

Jenna wanted to smile at this testy side of Riley.

"You sound like my grandmother.''

He rolled his eyes. "Terrific. Now you're trying to wrap me in a shawl and put me in a rocking chair.''

"Why? My grandmother started taking flying lessons when she was fifty and took up skiing when she was sixty. For her seventy-fifth birthday, she started skydiving. I can't imagine she's slowed down any since the last time I saw her.''

Riley didn't need any reminder of how much Jenna had given up when she entered the Witness Relocation Program.

"I really screwed up your life, didn't I?'' He made it more a fact, not a question.

Jenna shook her head as she framed his face with her hands. "I got a lot of practice with life drawing,'' she teased.

Just as she knew it would, Riley's face grew a dark red. She knew the man didn't have one inhibited bone in his body, but the times she talked him into posing for her showed her there were a few things he was uncomfortable doing. One of them was posing nude.

"If we're going we better get down to the lobby." Riley picked up his sunglasses and set a baseball cap on his head, pulling the bill down over his eyes.

Jenna picked up the hat she planned to wear when they reached their destination and followed him out of the bungalow.

When they reached the lobby, they found the tour group standing around in a loose group.

"Gee, I may have trouble finding you among all these clones," she murmured. She furtively eyed several of the men, who wore loud patterned shirts that matched their wives' tops. "On second thought, I won't have all that much trouble. We're almost the only ones not wearing matching shirts."

Riley eyed some of the more ostentatious floral print shirts worn by men and women alike. "No way you'll ever get me into one of those," he muttered.

"No problem. I'd never buy you one. Although that bright red and blue with all the parrots looks neat."

He grabbed her hand and pulled her outside. "Not in this lifetime."

The small bus the group was herded onto was modern and air-conditioned.

"All the comforts of home," Riley commented as he eased his seat back a bit. He picked up her hand and sandwiched it between his. He held it during the drive.

Since the seats were large enough, Jenna curled her legs up under her and to one side so she could

lean against Riley. He smiled and slipped an arm
around her shoulders. She snuggled up closer to him.

"It's a forty-minute ride, so you may as well make
yourself comfortable," he told her.

"Thank you, Riley," she murmured, turning her
head just enough to press a kiss against his neck. Her
breath was warm against his skin. "This will be a
wonderful day. I know it will."

He wanted to tell her not to thank him until they
were safely back at the bungalow. He wanted to tell
her he changed his mind and they weren't going,
after all. He wanted to tell her the jittery feeling he'd
been experiencing lately was increasing. He didn't
like it one bit. He felt as if he should be looking over
his shoulder all the time.

He told himself he had these odd feelings because
it had been way too quiet for too long. He told himself it was because he'd been out of the game, and
he worried his reflexes weren't what they were supposed to be.

You didn't have to worry about carrying a gun
when you were out surfing.

Most of all, he worried that all he would have to
do is make one tiny mistake and Jenna would be the
one to pay the hefty price.

With her life.

Chapter 10

"**W**hy didn't I wear my running shoes?" Jenna moaned as she followed Riley off the bus. She stopped for a second to slip off her sandals and knock the dirt out of them.

"Don't even think I'm going to carry you," Riley warned her.

He barely turned around when she suddenly leaped onto his back and wrapped her legs around his waist and her arms around his neck.

"You were saying?" she giggled.

Several others walking around them laughed at the stunned look on Riley's face.

"Why can't you be fun like that?" One blond woman asked the man she was with. The expression on his face told her that wasn't his idea of fun.

"Don't worry, baby, we'll have our own fun when we get back to the hotel," he promised her. "You

wanted to see these damn things, so let's get it over
with.''

Riley turned his head and stared at Jenna.

"Do not even think about dumping me," she
whispered in his ear, playfully pulling his hair.

Riley dutifully carried Jenna piggyback until they
reached the first temple. He loosened his hold, and
she hopped down. She pulled her camera out of her
tote bag and began snapping pictures.

"Look at this!" she enthused, holding the view-
finder up to her eye and tipping her head back to get
as much of the stone temple as she could. "We have
to climb this, Riley." She grabbed his hand and
pulled him toward the steep steps at one end of the
building.

He hung back. "Let's explore the interior first."

Jenna considered it and nodded.

The temple was surprisingly cool inside compared
to the heat outside.

Jenna was disappointed that there were no draw-
ings on the walls. She already knew there wouldn't
be any rare artifacts since the temple had been plun-
dered centuries ago and archeologists had taken the
rest. Instead she allowed her imagination to take over
and tell her what might have been found there.

She could see pots glazed with earthen colors set
in the niches carved within the walls. She wondered
if they would have had wall hangings depicting
scenes of daily life or religious rituals. Priests, wearing their garb of power, would be in here praying to
their gods and going about their daily duties. She felt
as if she could hear their chants echoing in her mind.

"How sad that there is so little known about these

people," she murmured, placing her hand against a wall and feeling the cool stone rough against her skin. "I wonder what their lives were like. Were they happy? Did they have large families? Did they have to work hard? What were their festivals like? Did they have enemies?"

"They probably had all of the above along with a few virgin sacrifices to spice up the holidays." Riley leaned down to murmur in her ear, "But then I guess you don't have to worry about that, do you?"

She not so subtly pushed her elbow into his stomach. "You don't have to gloat, you know."

He grunted from the contact. It turned out she had a very sharp elbow. "It's a guy thing."

"From what I remember, men were also sacrificed." Jenna grabbed his hand and pulled him back outside. "Maybe we'll find out once we've reached the top." She climbed up the first step and looked over her shoulder. "Are you coming?"

Riley sighed. "Not just yet. Maybe later." He climbed up after her.

Leaves rustled from the nearby jungle of thick plants and trees. Eyes hidden behind dark glasses scanned and counted the number of people walking around the small cluster of temples. They also tracked the others brave enough to climb up the main structure. The owner of the eyes didn't like what he saw.

There were too many people around for to him accomplish his task. Still, he was a professional. If he was patient he would have his opportunity. He wanted to be as far away as possible by nightfall.

He had to succeed. He was told not to come back until he accomplished the job.

He touched the knife strapped to his thigh.

He didn't like using guns. Never had. They were too impersonal. He preferred his work to be up close and personal. The only way he could do that was with a knife. Or his fists.

She had been afraid of him that night. She couldn't hide it. He drank in that fear as if it had been a strong narcotic. He liked knowing she was afraid of him. The power he'd had over her that night let him feel in control. He always liked being in control of a situation.

It was something he couldn't experience when he reported to his employer. He didn't know the man's name. The man had never introduced himself, and to be honest, he never wanted to know the bastard's name. He always had the feeling if he said one word wrong the man would kill him without a second thought. He considered himself a coldhearted bastard. He considered his employer a man who didn't have a heart.

If he could, he'd leave the man's employ and go elsewhere. He didn't care that the money was excellent. He'd rather work for anyone but the man he privately called the devil. There was only one problem.

The only resignation his employer would accept was death. His.

"What is it with you and climbing?" Riley grumbled, once they reached the top of the stone edifice.

"This is beautiful!" Jenna spun around with her arms open wide as if to accept the sun around her.

Jenna stopped when she found Riley watching her. It was too easy to forget they had been apart for some time. Here in Mexico she could make herself believe none of it had ever happened. She could believe they were down here for a once-in-a-lifetime vacation.

She wondered what Riley would do if she told him she never tired of looking at him. Even more so now.

He didn't have the short hair he'd had back then. The longer locks were always tied back with a strip of leather. Time had carved sharp lines in his features, but she still saw the same man she saw that first time—saw and fell in love with him two seconds later.

For three years Jenna had told herself she'd gotten Riley out of her system. She'd even convinced herself she was ready to get on with her life.

Then Riley showed up again at her request, and all his return did was teach her she still wasn't over him. He'd had her heart all this time.

No wonder no other man had a chance.

She boosted herself up onto the altar and sat there with her legs crossed Indian-style.

"I'd say it's more than big enough to hold a man for sacrifice," she announced, patting the stone top.

Riley walked over and braced his hands against the edge. "Naw, you look much better up there than I would. Of course, you'd have to wear a lot less."

"So would you." She traced the outline of his T-shirt neckline. "Your skin would be oiled and you'd wear feathers so you wouldn't be completely nude before the gods." Her lips curved upward. "Long feathers."

His eyes darkened with the same desire that glowed in her eyes. "You're just asking for it, aren't you?"

"Yes, but I have an idea you wouldn't be up to having an audience," she said in a low breathy voice that seemed to ooze sex.

Riley grabbed her around her waist and pulled her off the altar.

"Okay, Smitty, you've had your fun. Come on, let's get back down so the driver doesn't take off without us."

Jenna looked around as Riley dragged her back to the stairs.

"I bet this place would be fascinating on a night when there's a full moon."

"Only if you're into all that woo-woo stuff." He shook his head.

"I bet on a quiet night you can hear the drums and the priests chanting." She hopped down the stairs one at a time. "Then you'd hear the cries of the victims as the knife descends."

Riley stopped and pulled her to a stop. "When did you pick up this bloodthirsty nature?" he asked.

"I picked up a few books in the resort gift shop. It was very informative about the tribes that lived here centuries ago," she replied. She looked around with an expression on her face that could only be called wistful. Her whisper echoed the ache written on her face. "I wish I could draw all this. And use all the rich colors for that time period."

Riley felt her pain as if it was his own. He cocked

an elbow around her neck and drew her to him. He dropped a kiss on the top of her head.

"You will draw again," he assured her, gently rubbing his cheek against her hair. "I never had any doubts. You shouldn't, either."

She smiled up at him. "You're good for my ego, Riley."

Once they reached solid ground, Jenna looked around, whispered in Riley's ear and went off to her left.

"Don't go too far," he warned, beginning to follow her when an older man stopped him to ask a question.

Jenna wrinkled her nose at the pungent aroma of vegetation as she found a private spot. Afterward, her attention was caught by a large cluster of colorful blossoms.

She had just leaned down to carefully touch a blossom when a new smell reached her nostrils. This one had nothing to do with the lush vegetation around her. She stiffened as she identified it as one that brought back old nightmares.

She opened her mouth to scream Riley's name at the same moment a hand clapped over it.

Memories ran over her like molten lava as the scent of baby powder invaded her nostrils along with the sharper tang of licorice.

"You're lookin' real hot today, Jenna," the man whispered nastily in her ear. His other hand passed across her breasts then roughly pressed her against him.

She froze, afraid to do anything that might incite him.

"Have you missed me, Jenna?" His breath was hot and sour. "I've sure missed you. We had quite a time that night, didn't we?" He tightened his hold, deliberately pulling her up off her feet.

No! It's a nightmare! All I have to do is wake up and everything will be all right!

Her eyes frantically whipped right and left, hoping Riley would suddenly appear. Her assailant's callused hand was filthy, and she had to constantly swallow to keep from gagging.

Riley! Where are you? She hated the tears streaming down her cheeks.

"Don't worry, baby." His tongue snaked out and dipped in her tears. "I'll take really good care of you. Too bad I can't keep you for too long. But then, you knew that, didn't you?"

He's going to kill me. He didn't kill me last time, so he's going to do it this time.

She shifted her weight with the hope of stamping her foot on his, but he jerked her back so quickly her head snapped back and forth. A knife appeared in his hand, and the sharp blade rested against her throat.

"Don't try anything funny," he warned, barely pressing the knife down.

Jenna could feel the sting first, then a damp sensation, as a trickle of warm blood trailed down her neck.

She was helpless as he started walking backward, dragging her with him farther into the vegetation that quickly hid them from the group. She lashed out with her feet, but he was bigger and stronger than she was. She hated herself for tears that refused to stop.

This wasn't Riley's fault, she told herself. She

should have been more careful. Stayed closer to the group, even though it wouldn't have been easy. She was afraid he'd blame himself for what she'd done. She didn't want him feeling responsible for her death.

"Hey, buddy, don't you know it's against the law to take souvenirs out of the area. Something like that can get you in a lot of trouble."

Jenna's cries were muffled by the man's hand as he spun around with her limply hanging in his hold. He tightened his arm against her throat.

Riley stood nearby with his weapon in his hand. The look on his face said it all.

"You try to shoot me, she'll get her throat slit."

Jenna trembled as she heard the threat she already knew the man wouldn't hesitate to keep. She tried to use her eyes to communicate with Riley to no avail. He barely spared her a glance after he'd seen the trickle of blood marring her throat.

"She's a tasty piece, Cooper," the man snarled. "You've had your fun. Now it's my turn. But first, I'm gonna see you dead." He raised his free hand, revealing his knife. Before it could leave his hand, Riley's hand was up. The explosion sent birds screeching and wildly flying overhead.

Jenna screamed the moment the man's hand slid away from her face. She was blind to the world around her, and her ears rang from the gunshot that flew so close to her. She sank down to the ground, screaming even more when the man's arm flopped onto her leg. She tried to crawl away.

"Jen, you're okay. Everything's fine," Riley repeated in a calm voice that somehow managed to sound frantic at the same time. He wrapped his arms around her and held her tight against his chest.

"What happened?"

"Who's he?"

Riley looked up and found himself looking at four men. The driver also stood there. He carried a pistol, which he kept aimed at the man.

"This scum decided he wanted to take my woman," Riley muttered, still keeping a protective hold on Jenna.

One of the men moved closer and crouched down by the body. He pressed his fingers against the carotid artery.

"He's still alive."

"I want to know why he's out here," Riley said grimly.

One of the other men pulled out a cellular phone. "The hotel can pick him up."

"It was him. It was him," Jenna babbled, frantically pawing at Riley.

"I know, baby. I know," he soothed, gathering her hands in his. He freed one hand to press his handkerchief against the cut on her neck. He was relieved when the bleeding stopped and he could see the cut. It was shallow. He inwardly shuddered at what could have happened to her.

"Do you want something to calm her down?" A young blond woman held out a pill container.

Riley inwardly winced at the variety the woman carried.

"No, thanks. I'm just going to get her to the bus." He stood, pulling Jenna up with him. He swung her into his arms.

She closed her eyes and clung tightly to him.

"Don't say anymore, honey," he whispered. "We'll be back at the hotel in no time."

One of the men stopped Riley to tell him a couple of them would be staying behind to keep an eye on the wounded man. Riley knew he should stay in case the man regained consciousness, but he didn't want to leave Jenna. His heart was having a massive argument with his brain.

"You need to stay here, don't you?" Her chin trembled violently, tearstains streaked her cheeks, and her eyes were bright with fear. "You need to be here in case he comes to, you don't want anyone else questioning him, so you have to stay behind."

He nodded. Conflicting emotions raced across his face.

Jenna motioned for him to put her down. "Then you stay here. I'm sure I won't be in any danger on the bus going back to the hotel." Her voice wobbled tearfully again even as hysterical laughter tried to edge its way in. "Can you imagine anyone wanting to hijack the bus? Where would they go?"

Riley pulled Jenna to him and held on to her hard. Anyone who saw his face saw the conflicting emotions and the pain twisting him into knots inside.

"I'll make it as fast as I can," he promised, his voice was hard with conviction. "When you get back, ask for Sasha. Stay with him. He'll look after you."

Riley escorted Jenna to the bus and made sure she was all right before he left her. The woman who had offered Jenna a tranquilizer earlier promised to keep an eye on her.

"He's really cute," she told Jenna as she settled into the seat beside her as the driver started the engine. "My Andy stayed behind to help. I tell you, it's not safe anywhere. Andy said we could have a great honeymoon down here and party. Now some creep shows up and ruins the whole thing."

Jenna turned away to look out the window. She wasn't sure whether to burst out laughing or crying at the woman's glib comment. She wanted to tell her the day wouldn't have been just ruined. If the man had succeeded, Jenna would have been very much dead.

Riley didn't want to let Jenna out of his sight. But he knew he couldn't keep her with him. She needed to get away from here right away. And he trusted Sasha to take good care of her until he got back to the hotel.

Two men stayed behind with him. Andrew, a contractor from Detroit who was there on his honeymoon. And Marcus, a stockbroker from Texas, who'd brought his wife for a second honeymoon after the birth of their second child.

"Looks as if the bleeding stopped," Andrew commented. He absently nudged the unconscious man with the toe of his shoe. "What do you think he wanted with your wife?"

"Hell if I know," Riley muttered the lie without a second thought. He frowned as he studied their prisoner. "Maybe he grabbed her because she had wandered away from the group and he figured her for an easy mark. Dammit, I told her to stay close by! I only turned away for a second.'' He took a deep breath.

Marcus shook his head. ''Who knows what he was after. He doesn't look like he belongs around here.''

Riley crouched down and began searching through the man's pockets. He doubted he would find anything useful, but he could hope.

Other than a vehicle key and a wallet containing cash, no other identification was found.

''I wonder where he left his truck,'' Andrew stated, looking around. ''He couldn't have left it too far away. I'll go see if I can find it.''

Riley would have liked that privilege himself, but he also knew he couldn't do everything. He could only hope there wasn't anything about Jenna or him to be found in the vehicle.

''I'd appreciate that.''

''It could have been my wife.'' Andrew clapped him on the back. ''Give a shout when someone from the hotel shows up.'' He made a circle around them, examined the ground and headed off.

Marcus shook his head. ''This isn't good.''

Riley shot him a sharp look. ''I know I'd like to find out how he got here and why he's here.''

'' 'Why' is a good question to ask. Obviously he thought he could catch some rich tourists.''

Riley froze momentarily when the man on the ground moved his head and moaned. His eyelids fluttered but didn't open. Riley thought of the fear that had left Jenna a quivering mass.

The man had held her intimately, touched her. A savage anger welled up inside him, and for a moment he wanted nothing more than to kill the man with his bare hands.

"Let's just hope he comes to long enough to answer some questions," he said in a hard voice. "I want the chance to find out what he thought he was doing."

When a small pickup arrived, Riley and Marcus lifted the still-unconscious man and laid him in the back of the truck. The driver leaned on the horn several times and after a while, Andrew appeared.

"I found an old Jeep about two miles from here," he announced. "I took it apart as much as I could, but I couldn't find anything. Not even a rental agreement. He wake up?"

The two men shook their heads.

By now Riley was eager to get back to the hotel. And back to Jenna.

The ride back was bumpy, with the prisoner moaning in pain more than once when they hit a pothole. Riley sat in the back of the truck as did Andrew while Marcus sat with the driver. The two men were silent during the ride back as if each was buried in his own thoughts.

When they arrived at the hotel, the driver guided the truck to the rear of the main building and explained he would take the wounded man down to the infirmary. He was certain the hotel would call the authorities. Riley didn't want that done, but he figured Sasha would already know that.

Riley thanked the other two men for their help and said drinks were definitely on him. For now, he wanted to see if he could find anything out.

He impatiently waited while the doctor examined

his new patient. The man brusquely ordered a nurse to prepare for surgery.

"You won't learn anything from this man today," he told Riley.

"If he wakes up, I want to be called immediately," he said grimly.

"You will." The doctor's smile softened. "I was summoned to your bungalow when your wife returned."

"Is she all right?" he asked sharply.

"Shaken, of course, but physically, she is fine. The cut on her throat was superficial. One meant to look more dangerous than it was. There will be no scar."

Riley nodded at the doctor's reassurances, although all he cared about was that Jenna was all right.

"I left a sedative for her in case she becomes agitated in the night. Sometimes, it takes the body closing down for the brain to relive those fears," he explained.

"Thank you."

Riley left as quickly as he could and headed for the bungalow. When he entered the parlor he found Sasha seated in a chair reading.

Riley had to smile at seeing the elderly man sporting a pair of old-fashioned reading glasses and reading a book of Russian poetry.

Sasha looked up and removed his glasses. "She is asleep. Is the man alive?"

Riley nodded. "The doctor is going to take out the bullet now. He said not to worry about him until tomorrow. I told him I wanted to know the minute he woke up."

"I want to be with you when you interrogate him. This man attacked a guest of my resort. I wish to know how he managed to find out when the tour group would be at the temple. It worries me to think one of my people would give him that kind of information," Sasha said sharply as he placed a bookmark in his book before closing it.

"The driver figured someone would be calling the authorities," Riley said.

Sasha nodded. "But it will take time for someone to show up."

Riley felt very tired. The adrenaline he'd been running on for the past few hours was rapidly leaving his body.

"You have a woman with a great heart and much courage. Cherish her, my friend. Women like her are very rare." Sasha patted his shoulder as he walked past.

The moment the door closed after the older man, Riley was inside the bedroom to check on Jenna.

She lay curled up under the covers. Her respiration was normal, and she didn't appear to be having any bad dreams.

Riley wanted nothing more than to lie down beside her and take her in his arms. He wanted the assurance of her body nestled against his. He needed to know she was all right. But he also knew a shower would be in order first.

Then he'd do just what Sasha suggested.

He'd cherish Jenna for all he was worth.

Chapter 11

Jenna's first thoughts when she woke up were those of unceasing terror. It was as if the past days hadn't happened. She was back in that monstrous world of pain again.

She sat up in bed feeling horror clawing at her throat. The sounds coming from her were unintelligible as she blindly fought the monsters terrorizing her. She lashed out with all her strength, needing to fight back even if she was rewarded with more pain.

She was so lost in her nightmare, she barely felt the pair of arms warmly surround her. Once she realized whose arms were wrapped around her, she grew limp in his embrace.

She opened her eyes and drew in deep breaths to help clear her mind. She turned her head to see it was dark outside.

Riley had obviously left on a lamp in the parlor

that sent a soft yellow glow streaming through the open doorway and across their bed.

A rough palm warmly caressed her cheek.

"You okay?" His voice was soft and comforting to her frazzled mind.

She nodded as words still failed her. She remained curled up against him with her cheek resting against his chest.

"Sasha's idea of comfort is to swallow a glass of vodka," she whispered. "Do you know what straight vodka tastes like?" She didn't wait for him to answer. "It tastes like lava straight out of the volcano. It's disgusting. I think it was really a Russian Mickey Finn."

"That's a new way of putting it," he said softly.

She tilted her head back so she could face him.

"He was the one from before," she whispered. "How did he find us, Riley? We should have been safe here."

"I don't know," he whispered back. "He's been unconscious since we brought him back, so I haven't been able to get any answers from him. He was taken into surgery right away and hasn't come out of the anesthesia yet. I told the doctor to call me when he wakes up."

"Do you think he'll tell you how Grieco hired him?"

"He may not want to, but I think we can persuade him to tell me what I want to know."

Jenna's brow furrowed in thought. "Will you hurt him?"

He hesitated. "Smitty."

"No, let me finish. I want you to hurt him," she

said hurriedly. "I want you to tie electrodes to sensitive parts of his body and turn on the juice. Hang him upside down by his toes. Put him in a pool filled with piranha or hungry sharks. Maybe stake him over an anthill and cover him with honey." It was clear she was getting into her element.

Riley winced. "Where did you learn all this? I can't imagine your local night school offered Torture 101 as one of its classes."

"I watched a lot of B movies the nights I couldn't sleep," she admitted. "I just don't want to know that you're going to sit there and ask him questions and he'll sit there and just stare at you."

Riley grinned. "You're a bloodthirsty wench, Smitty."

She shook her head. "Only when it comes to him. Just make him suffer."

He brushed her hair away from her eyes. "Be careful, Jen. What you want is the same as what he does for a living. Once you start down that road it isn't easy to find your way back."

She shifted her body, burrowing farther under the covers. "Is that what happened to you? You were afraid you couldn't find your way back?"

"Close enough."

"Is that one of the reasons you left the Marshal's Service?"

The question hung in the air between them for so long Jenna didn't expect him to answer her.

"I left because I felt I could no longer effectively do my job," he said finally.

It was as if the partial darkness gave them per-

mission to discuss what had been kept quiet for so
long.

"Because of me?"

"Because I knew every day I'd go in to work I'd
want to look through the computer and find out
where you were. I'd want to know all about your
new life. For all I knew, I'd even travel to wherever
you were while lying to myself and saying I was only
doing it because I wanted to know you were safe,"
he said candidly. "What I felt was wrong. That's
when I decided it was time to get out."

"Where did you go?"

"I have a house on the far shore on the island of
Kauai. It's not much more than a beach shack, but
it's fine for me." He sounded as if he was speaking
the truth, but there was still a ring of some undefin-
able emotion in his words.

The pain was stark in Jenna's eyes. She had left
Riley because she felt she was doing something for
his own good. Instead, he'd gone on to make a life
without her. While he hadn't said anything, she
sensed he'd been living only a half life the same way
she had. She always felt as if she'd been waiting for
something very special.

It sounded as if he'd been merely existing, too.

Was that why she called for Riley when she lay
in the hospital that night? Why she refused to see,
or talk, to anyone else? They'd told her he was no
longer with the Marshal's Service. She hadn't cared.
She only wanted him.

Now she could be honest with herself. She hadn't
wanted Riley to come to her because she knew he
would keep her safe. That wasn't the only reason.

She wanted Riley because she hadn't stopped loving him. She wanted to see him again. She didn't care how selfish her demands were.

She reached out and touched his cheek with her fingertips. The pads lightly traced the harsh lines, feeling the sandpapery texture of his skin.

"I wouldn't have needed the sand and the water as long as I had you," she murmured. "What I always needed was you, Riley."

His eyes flared with raw emotion as her words wrapped themselves around him.

"But I knew how much you loved your work. It wasn't right for me to insist you give it up." She continued stroking his face, retracing the familiar contours. "What you've said is I made the wrong choice. Just consider that I was afraid to discuss it with you. Especially after…" Her voice dropped off.

Riley didn't need to hear the words to know what she meant. Their argument about babies. The night he'd found the pregnancy test box. The night that she later wished she hadn't gone into work. What would have happened if she had been home when he arrived? Could she have staved off his finding the box, and life would have gone on as before?

Those were all thoughts she didn't want to pursue because she never felt she had the right answers.

"Afraid?" He showed surprise at her choice of words. "Why were you afraid? I know I acted pretty much like an idiot that night, but you still didn't need to be afraid of me."

"I didn't want you to hate me later for taking you away from what you knew and loved," she admitted

in a soft voice. "You know that's why I had to
leave."

"Oh, Smitty." His voice ached with so many
emotions they overflowed. He cupped her cheek with
his palm and lowered his head until his lips touched
hers in the barest of kisses. "There was nothing,
nothing, that mattered to me as much as you did. I
would have killed Grieco with my bare hands before
I would have allowed him to lay a finger on you. I
wanted to kill that bastard out there today. I might
even have done it if we hadn't had an audience. I
wanted to hurt him the way he hurt you." His breath
was warm against her lips.

She kept her arms around his neck, so he couldn't
move away from her

"You're an honorable man, Riley Cooper," she
brushed her lips against his. "Ask Sasha to use the
electrodes and the bamboo shoots under the finger-
nails."

It was as simple as his slowly sliding over her, his
knee nudging hers apart as he settled himself in the
cradle of her thighs. Her short nightgown hitched up
to her waist as he spread his palm across her flat
belly.

At the same time her own hand moved across his
shoulder. Her fingers traced a scar she knew came
from a knife wound about six years ago. She found
another scar that was round and puckered along his
side. When her hand crossed his washboard belly, he
sucked in a deep breath at her light touch.

He touched her as she touched him.

His fingers tangled in the dark blond hair at her
apex, his finger gently probing the moist folds. One

finger entered, a second followed to rub the tiny nub nestled there.

Jenna gasped and arched upward.

Riley's head moved downward until his mouth covered her breast. His fingers danced inside her as he suckled on her taut nipple. He could sense her heart racing, hear her frenzied whimpers as she began to thrash under him. He ignored her murmured pleas and continued taking her higher. As he felt her start to tighten and tremble, he lifted his head. He ignored her whimpered cries and quickly slid downward until his mouth replaced his fingers.

Jenna's eyes snapped wide-open as his hot moist breath seared ultrasensitive tissue. She moaned his name as he drank deeply from her. His probing tongue drove her even higher until she was wound as tight as a wire.

Riley felt no pain as her nails dug deeply into his shoulders. He held her hips fast as he kept on sending her further into space.

It was as if Riley knew exactly where Jenna was. What she was feeling. How much more she could take. Just as abruptly he lifted his head and pulled himself up over her. It seemed a lifetime as he hastily rolled on protection even if it was only scant seconds. He thrust deeply into her with a powerful stroke that sent her over the edge.

Jenna's scream of release was swallowed by his covering mouth. She was so lost in acute sensations that she could only wrap her legs around him and hang on. She was lost, but she wanted him to feel the extreme pleasure she did. She reached down between them and touched him. His expletive described where they were, just as he released himself into her.

They wrapped their arms around each other, remaining that way as they fought to catch their breath.

"Tell me, Smitty, are you going to respect me in the morning?"

"Is respect that important to you?" Jenna asked, her voice shaking with suppressed laughter.

"Yes, it is," he said solemnly.

Riley dropped light kisses across her forehead and along one temple.

"I don't want people to think I'm easy," he murmured. "After all, I have feelings, too."

Jenna pasted a properly contrite expression on her face. "I wouldn't dream of hurting your feelings, Riley," she told him. "Of course I will hold you in the highest respect."

They stared at each other with solemn gazes until Jenna finally broke down laughing.

"Great way to make me feel better, Smitty," Riley grumbled.

Jenna opened her mouth to reply when the phone rang. Both froze. Riley kissed her and kept one arm around her as he rolled over and snagged the receiver.

"Yeah?" He settled the receiver between his shoulder and his ear.

"Such lovely telephone manners," Jenna murmured. "Is that what you learned as a marshal? How to intimidate someone in one word."

Riley listened for several minutes. "I'll be there in ten minutes." He hung up.

"He's awake," she guessed.

He nodded at her statement. He climbed out of bed and headed for the bathroom.

Jenna lay back, listening to the sounds of the shower running. Riley came back out of the bathroom with his still-wet hair slicked back from his face. He pulled on shorts and a T-shirt then looked at her as if he'd suddenly remembered she was in the room.

"I don't want you leaving here until I get back. Will you do that for me?"

She nodded. A trace of fear crossed her face. "You'll be careful, won't you?"

Riley walked over to the bed and leaned down, kissing her deeply until she was breathless.

"Don't worry. He'll be so pumped up with pain-killers he won't be able to even lift his little finger."

"Then he might not remember his own name, either," she said worriedly.

He kissed her again. "I'll see you later."

Jenna watched him leave the room. She was still worried about him seeing that man again, but she didn't doubt Riley would learn something.

"My hero," she murmured.

Riley couldn't remember ever being in a hospital that didn't smell of antiseptic and sorrow. That was probably why he stayed out of them as much as possible.

This one smelled more like French vanilla along with the homey aroma of French roast coffee drifting down the hallway.

"The patient is doing well," Dr. Minton reported to Riley and Sasha, who'd joined him. "He was bewildered when he woke up and demanded to know where he was. The nurse told him he had just had surgery and was now in a medical facility. He has asked her a lot of questions, but she told him nothing more."

Riley looked at the older man. "Is there any way I can talk you out of coming with me?"

He smiled. "Of course not. This man has attacked one of the hotel's guests. I would like to know why."

"You're not alone on that score," Riley said grimly, heading for the door.

When Riley entered the room, he found a nurse with a book in her hand seated in a chair in the corner.

The man he'd shot was lying in the only bed in the room. He had one wrist handcuffed to the bed frame.

Riley glanced at the nurse. "We'd like to be alone with the patient."

The nurse quietly left the room and closed the door behind her.

"So, how're you feeling, sport?" Riley asked in an old-pal voice.

He snagged the chair the nurse had vacated and passed it to Sasha. He took the other chair and turned it around, sitting on it with his arms crossed along the back.

The man watched them warily.

"Sorry I had to shoot you, but hell, you were holding on to my woman. You were promising to hurt her. Even kill her. There was no way I could let you get away with that," Riley went on in his good-ole-boy manner. "You've got to consider yourself lucky you could get such excellent medical care so fast. This place is so isolated, who knows how long it would have taken to get you to a doctor. Of course, since we've helped you, it's only fair you help us out.''

"I've got nothing to tell you," he said sullenly.

"Would it be so bad to tell us your name?"

The man started to laugh then coughed. He winced in pain. "John Smith."

"Really? I've met a lot of your relatives. Popular name."

Riley linked his hands together in front of him. "So tell me, John. What brought you to these parts? I can't imagine you'd come all the way down here for some camping. Too many creatures that only come out at night. And the temple is pretty far out there. Considering you'd grabbed my woman, I guess you weren't out there to see the sights. You didn't have a camera on you nor was there one in your Jeep. Why don't you tell me why you were out there, John. Why did you cut my woman? Threaten to kill her.''

"I've got nothing to say." He looked away.

"You were on private land, Mr. Smith," Sasha spoke up. "This is land where trespassers have been shot without a second thought. It was by Ryan's good graces you were brought here and given medical treatment." He leaned forward, resting his hands on the engraved top of his cane.

Riley directed a level gaze at the man. "Personally, I'd like to spend some quality time with you. The same kind of quality time you spent with my lady. Of course, I'm bigger than she is, and I'd be more prone to fight back in a much nastier method.

And right now, you're feeling pretty crappy, so that should make it like it was with her. I'd start thinking about what you did to her and I'd lose my patience and it could come out worse for you. But what the hell. What goes around and all that, right?"

The man stiffened, and for a moment his shackled wrist fought the restraint. Pain crossed his face, and he fell back against the pillows.

"Who sent you out here, John?" Riley asked.

"You don't scare me." He glared at Sasha next. "Neither do you."

"What about your employer? How do you feel about him?" Sasha asked.

"He don't scare me."

Riley's interest was caught now. The man's words said one thing, but he saw a hint of fear in his eyes. The man wasn't as confident as he professed to be.

Riley knew this was the time for him to press his advantage. He wanted information from this man, and he intended to do whatever was necessary to get it.

"You know what, John? I think your boss does scare you. I also think he told you not to come back until you got the job done. And if you didn't get the job done, he'd want to cut you up into little pieces and feed you to his goldfish. Look what happened. You not only screwed up the job, but you got shot up. We've got you by the *cojones,* my friend. Your best bet would be to come clean. Tell us what we want to know and we can help you out."

"And if I don't talk?"

Riley didn't say anything. He just stared at the man for a moment. He knew the man lying on the bed was a professional. That was the only way he could have tracked them down here. He had just listened to his death sentence and barely batted an eye.

"Which one of Grieco's men hired you, John?" he asked abruptly.

"Grieco?" He laughed then coughed. "Everyone knows Grieco's in prison. His business went bust more than a year ago."

Riley froze. "What?"

"You heard me. His men fought over the business. Some ended up dead. A few are in prison and someone else took over."

Riley's brain whirled. "Who?"

"I don't know."

He refused to believe what he'd just heard. He talked to Dave every two days, and his former partner hadn't relayed any of that information.

"Why isn't word about it on the street?"

"There was some who wanted it kept quiet. They figured if it was too widely known there'd be even more fighting for it. That's all I know. I don't deal in the areas he did." He showed his distaste.

"No, you deal in the areas where you can beat up women." Riley stood up and left his chair. He walked over to the bed and leaned over. "I know what you did, John," he spoke in a whisper that seemed to slice through the other man. "You kept all the lights off and grabbed her when she walked into her apartment, didn't you? You knew she wouldn't put up much of a fight, because she didn't know how. I just want to know one thing. Who told you to break her fingers?" His dark eyes took on an unearthly glow. "Who told you to do that, John?"

His voice softened, but the fury was there. The need to hurt someone vibrated in his tone. His fingers tightened on the railing as if he had them wrapped around the other man's throat.

John tried to shy away from Riley, but there was nowhere for him to go.

"Did you know she was an artist at one time, John?" Riley continued speaking in a deadly soft voice. "She could paint pictures that would make your heart cry. Now it isn't known if she'll ever be able to paint again. Someone told you to break her fingers. Someone wanted her to suffer for the rest of her life. They wanted to make sure she couldn't return to her art." He leaned down until his face was close to John's. "She has the heart of an artist. She couldn't hurt a fly. But you took that away from her. Do you know what she wanted me to do to you, John?" He didn't bother waiting for an answer. "This sweet wonderful woman who wouldn't step on a bug asked me to consider using electrodes and medieval torture instruments on you." The man paled even more. "Make it easy on yourself, John. Tell me who hired you."

John looked frantically at Sasha as if for assistance. "If I tell you what you want to know I won't be able to hide anywhere in the world," he argued, fear making his gaze wild. "You don't know this man. He has people everywhere. He'd find me and kill me in ways even you couldn't imagine."

"I can make it simple for you, John. Tell me about your boss, and I'll make sure you'll never have to worry about him." His voice beckoned to the man, offering safety.

"Sure, you would," he scorned. "You want me dead for what I did to her. I'll tell you, and you'll still kill me. He wanted you dead, so why should you care what happens to me," he argued. "All I was told was to rough up the woman. He figured you'd come out of hiding once you heard she'd been attacked. He'd done what he could and couldn't find you. He knew the two of you were lovers and he was able to track her down."

Riley couldn't help it. He grabbed the front of the man's hospital gown and pulled him upward.

"*Who?* Who wanted me so bad he'd have you beat up a defenseless woman?" he growled, shaking the man. "So help me, if you don't give me the bastard's name, I'll feed you to the fishes."

"He'll kill me!"

"He won't have to, John, because I'll kill you first." Riley's grip on the man's hospital gown tightened.

The man looked into Riley's eyes. He could no longer succeed in his assignment which signed his death warrant with one man. It didn't matter because he read his own death on this man's face.

Chapter 12

Jenna hated waiting. It reminded her too much of the hours she'd spent waiting at the courthouse before she had to testify. Memories of hours waiting in small rooms with an armed U.S. Marshal by her side flooded her brain.

This time was even worse because she was waiting for Riley. She had no idea how long she'd waited, because she refused to look at the clock. Seeing the minutes pass by so slowly only made it worse.

She lay in bed trying to relax but couldn't. She filled the bathtub with hot water and laced it with bath oil with the idea of relaxing there.

Except every time she closed her eyes, she saw her attacker's face. Reading was out as was watching television. She paced the length of the parlor, all the time wishing she smoked so she could have something to do with her hands.

She jumped and exhaled a soft scream when the door opened and Riley stepped in.

"Who were you expecting? Dracula?" He grinned.

Jenna ran over to him and quickly examined his hands and arms.

"I didn't hurt him, Smitty," he said softly.

"I hate that nickname." She sniffed, feeling as if she was going to cry.

"No, you don't." He gathered her into his arms and rested his chin on top of her head. "I always thought it fit you."

She hugged him tightly around the waist because she needed the contact. "Tell me you put electrodes on his body and made him miserable."

"I told him you wanted me to use medieval torture instruments. He got so scared he talked before I had to bring out the rack and iron maiden," he assured her.

Jenna tipped her head back in order to look up at him. "Then he told you where to find Grieco's men."

He blew out the breath he'd been holding.

"He doesn't work for Grieco, Smitty."

She broke out of his embrace. "What do you mean he doesn't work for Grieco?" Her voice rose. "Why did he come after me, then?"

He looked as if he wished he was anywhere but here. "He came after you because the person he was really after was me, even the first time."

Jenna dropped unsteadily onto the nearest chair before her knees gave out. She kept shaking her head as if she couldn't believe what she was hearing.

"What do you mean?" she asked, still unable to comprehend what she just heard. "If he was after you, why did he come after me? I don't understand how he could even find me. I would think it would have been easier to find you than to go to so much trouble going after me."

Riley shook his head. "I guess I wasn't all that easy to find. I don't own a phone, and I keep to myself. I didn't want anyone to track me down so I covered my tracks pretty well after I resigned. I guess I did a better job of it than I realized."

Jenna looked away. She couldn't keep the pain from etching lines on her features.

"Yes, you must have done a wonderful job. Obviously better than the Marshal's Service did for me."

"This man's employer had a connection in the Service that he used. The connection had access to relocation records since he worked in that department. Obviously, he was able to get the information he was paid for," Riley explained. "After the man's employer got it, he had the man killed." Jenna winced. "It seems he never likes to leave any loose ends. Plus, he probably knew I'd find out who leaked the information and I'd kill him."

She shuddered at his grim words. There was no doubt he would have carried through and made sure the man didn't live another day.

"It's sad when a man values money over his principles," she murmured.

"He probably got what he deserved." Riley paced the length of the room. He looked deep in thought.

Jenna sat huddled in the chair not sure whether to

be afraid or relieved the man who had attacked her was caught. Because, either way, she knew it wasn't over for them.

Now Riley had to find the man who wanted him dead, and he had to do it before he, himself, ended up the victim.

She rested her chin on her drawn-up knees and silently regarded Riley. His body was taut and he couldn't seem to stop pacing back and forth across the room.

"What are we going to do?" she whispered.

It was several moments before Riley answered her.

"We're going to do what I should have had us do more than a week ago. We're going to get out of here," he said. He rubbed his hand over his jaw in thought. "Boss man knows where we are, and once he doesn't hear from his errand boy, he'll send someone else down here. Next time we might not be so lucky."

He dropped into a chair and buried his face in his hands. He swore long and hard under his breath. Most of it was directed at himself.

Jenna imagined she could feel the pain Riley was experiencing. She pushed herself off her chair and went to his side. She knelt on the floor and placed her hands on his knees. Her lips were close to his ear as she spoke softly.

"I shouldn't have insisted Dave find you for me. If you hadn't come, he would have lost."

He lifted his head and turned his head to look at her. "I don't know who this bastard is, but I do know one thing. Anyone who would order to have you so badly hurt, would not hesitate in ordering your death,'' he said flatly. ''He knew if I didn't show up because you were injured that I would go after him with a vengeance if you were killed.''

She blinked to keep back the tears, but it wasn't easy. His life was more at risk than hers was.

''This is all my fault. I was selfish. I wanted you with me because I wanted to feel safe,'' she told him. ''I've always felt safe with you. That you would protect me.'' She touched her fingertips to his lips when he started to speak. ''I knew better than to put you on a pedestal. You have the scars to prove you're not indestructible.'' She lightly touched a puckered scar on his upper arm just below his tattoo.

''I never considered myself indestructible,'' he admitted. ''My work was unpredictable, so I was always careful.''

''Then I came along and fell right into your world,'' Jenna teased gently, lifting her hand to brush a stray lock of hair from his forehead. ''Am I going to have to cheer you up right now, Riley? Or can you do it on your own?''

Riley reached down and hauled her into his lap. He held on to her tightly as if he was afraid she would suddenly disappear into thin air.

''I don't want anything to happen to you.'' His words were muffled against the curve of her neck. ''You've let me bully you and drag you down here without a word of explanation. I had Sassy give you a makeover and—''

''And you showed me that you hadn't forgotten me, and you made glorious love to me that echoes all the colors in the rainbow,'' she said. ''Should I start packing?''

He exhaled a deep breath.

"You may as well. I'm going to see what I can arrange for transportation." He didn't move.

Jenna wasn't about to protest. She was reluctant to leave the protection of his arms. She kept her cheek against the warm strength of his chest and just held on to him.

No matter what, they were together and would stay together until this was settled.

If either of them hoped for more than that, they didn't speak of it.

Riley knew preparations had to be made fast. He didn't think John Smith's employer would be too patient once he didn't hear from his employee.

Before leaving the resort, he stopped by the infirmary but was told the man snuck out during the night. Riley instinctively knew that all the man cared about now was saving his own life, and he wouldn't be coming after them.

Jenna could feel that Riley's senses were on alert as they entered the terminal. As he checked them in, she covertly scanned times for other outgoing flights. If she could find a way to sneak on one of them, she could be gone before he'd know it. She couldn't be a pawn in this deadly game, and he would be safe.

"I need to use the rest room," she murmured as they headed for their gate. "Why don't I meet you at the gate. I'll be fine."

Riley hesitated.

"Please, Riley, I'll be fine. It's only two gates down." She pushed him. "Go."

Once inside the rest room, she pulled off her cap

and fluffed her hair with her fingertips. She added a bright color of lipstick and shrugged on a T-shirt she had in her bag. After she added sunglasses, she checked her reflection in the mirror. Not a big change, but enough.

"Forget it, Smitty."

She spun around at the sound of a familiar voice.

"What are you doing? You're in the ladies' room," she hissed.

"What I'm doing is making sure you don't do anything stupid. How did you think you could sneak onto another flight? What were you going to use? With what, your smile?" He grabbed her hand and practically dragged her outside. "Now you're getting your butt on that plane, and you will not say one word," he ordered her in a low, fierce voice. "Do you hear me?"

She looked up. Her gaze was steady and not the least bit intimidated by his temper.

"You'd do better without me."

"I said, *do you hear me?*"

She didn't look at him as they walked swiftly down the aisle. "Loud and clear."

Jenna didn't say another word during the long flight to Houston. Once they arrived, Riley made a random pick of airlines and chose a flight that would be leaving within the half hour.

By the time they reached the destination Riley had in mind, they'd taken four flights, crossing several states.

Jenna was exhausted from their nonstop traveling. She was angry with Riley for dragging her from one state to another. And now she was cold. Her clothing, which was suitable for a southern climate, wasn't warm enough when they finally arrived at the Denver airport.

Riley put his arm around her shoulders. She was too grateful for his extra warmth to shrug him off.

"Do not ask me to get on another plane. There's no way I can even get close to one," she said wearily. "So help me, if you try to drag me on one, I will scream."

"Don't worry, we're finished with the flying part."

"That's good because I—what do you mean finished with the flying part?" she whined.

Riley shook his head and guided her to a rental car desk.

Within moments they were settled in a four-wheel-drive vehicle. Riley turned the heat on high while Jenna curled up into a tiny ball in the passenger seat.

"Now what?" she asked wearily, closing her eyes.

"Now we work on blending in," he replied, speeding up.

Riley drove until he reached a mall. He found a parking spot near a door and pulled in.

"We should be able to find everything we need," he told her as he led her inside.

"Right now long underwear sounds wonderful."

Jenna was tired, but the idea of shopping was a nice pick-me-up.

With Riley and his credit cards on her heels she turned into a woman on a mission.

She wasted no time in choosing jeans, corduroy pants, sweaters, warm tops and a coat. Then she went on to select underwear and shoes. Riley didn't look pleased at the flannel nightgowns, but didn't say a word.

After she finished she followed him to the men's department where Riley made his own purchases.

Pleading hunger, Jenna was able to convince Riley to stop long enough to eat. When they walked back outside, she was relieved to have her heavy coat, boots, gloves and woolen cap to battle the freezing cold.

"Are you going to tell me where we're going next?" she demanded.

"You'll find out soon enough," he said cryptically as he assisted her into the passenger seat.

"I liked it better when we hid out in a warm climate," she muttered, scrunching down in her seat with her legs curled under her.

"That's the way it goes," he murmured, pulling out onto the highway.

Not long after, he noticed Jenna had fallen asleep. Her coat billowed out around her, and for a moment he swore she looked as she would if she were pregnant. He thought of her body ripe with his child. The idea of her having his child was heart stopping. He could see a little girl with Jenna's delicate features that would know how to wrap him around her tiny fingers. A little boy who ran reckless because he knew no fear. But since he bore his mother's eyes, he could do no wrong.

It was a future he didn't dare plan for himself. But now it was a future he figured it wouldn't hurt to dream about.

Something fierce welled up inside him, and his

hold on the steering wheel tightened as pictures of babies flashed before his eyes.

He knew he had to get this situation settled fast. He refused to think she might pay the price because of him.

He thought of his emotionally scarred childhood that left him not wanting to be that kind of father to a child. Not wanting to put any child through that kind of hell. It was a vow he'd made as a young man and a vow he refused to break.

What he hadn't counted on was Jenna coming into his life. He thought of finding the home pregnancy test kit in what seemed so many eons ago. Jenna, softly rounded with his child, had come into his head at that time. And, for a scant second, it hadn't seemed so bad. Until the memory of his vow had intruded with head-banging clarity.

Maybe he was finally seeing things differently.

Fate seemed to enjoy playing tricks on him. It threw him with Jenna again. He learned he could never forget her because she had always been a part of him. She carried his heart.

And if he had an ounce of sense, after all this was over, she'd carry his child.

Jenna was still sound asleep when Riley parked the vehicle by a boat dock. He kept the motor running so she could stay warm while he unloaded their packages. He carried them down to the end of the dock and placed them in a speedboat moored there. Once they were loaded, he returned to the truck for Jenna. He carefully picked her up so as not to awaken her and carried her over to the sleek speed-boat.

Riley looked around at the barren landscape. It was exactly what they needed.

He made sure Jenna was secure on a cushioned bench before he sat behind the boat controls. She mumbled something incoherent and settled back to sleep.

The boat ride was wet and cold. Riley didn't flinch against the icy spray hitting his face as he guided the boat across the lake. He knew the first thing he'd have to do is get hold of Dave and tell him they'd moved.

He hadn't been able to reach the man before he'd left Mexico. John Smith claimed the marshal who'd leaked the information was dead. That didn't mean there wasn't someone else working for John's boss, and Riley wanted Dave to check into that.

Damn, he felt so powerless! He looked down to see his hand clenched in a tight fist.

Riley was used to wading right into the thick of things. He was a man of action. Sitting around and waiting for something to happen wasn't his style.

Oh, he'd had more than his share of sitting at stakeouts. He considered it an activity equal to watching grass grow. And he'd drawn his share of watching over witnesses. But he still preferred being out there doing something.

This time was harder for him. He vowed he would protect Jenna with his life. But he wanted to be the one to be out there and do all the dirty work. He wanted to make sure no one would ever come after her again.

He'd had no idea that meant someone would use her to get to him.

He thought back to the first time he'd seen her—standing by the road. She was furious with her date for driving off.

If he knew then what he knew now would he have settled for politely assisting her and never seeking her again?

That was a question he didn't want to answer. Because the answer he *should* give would be a lie.

He couldn't afford to lose her again.

Chapter 13

Jenna woke up feeling disoriented after her long nap. She found herself lying on a bed with a soft flannel quilt placed over her. Her coat and shoes had been removed along with her sweater and jeans. She sat up and pushed her hair away from her eyes as she narrowed her eyes in the dim light.

"I see you finally decided to join us. Want some?" A cup filled with aromatic coffee was passed under her nose.

She grasped the mug with both hands and carefully sipped the hot liquid.

"I gather you undressed me."

"Nah, I let the butler do it. I figured it was his job. He hasn't seen a female in a good thirty years, so he was real eager to help out." The harsh lines in Riley's face smoothed out with his grin.

She shot him her "I am not amused" look.

"So who made the coffee? You or the butler? Please don't tell me his name is Jeeves."

"There's just us. The place may look rustic, but it's got all the comforts of home. We've got central heating, central air, indoor plumbing and a fully stocked kitchen. Along with a satellite dish out back, one of those theater-size television screens in the family room and an incredible video library. I don't know about you, but I could easily live here." Riley sat on the edge of the bed.

Jenna looked at him. He was now warmly dressed in jeans and a green marled-yarn sweater. She sipped her coffee some more before setting her cup aside.

"Who owns this getaway paradise?"

"A friend who won't mind our camping out here for a while," Riley said glibly.

Since Jenna still wasn't fully awake, it took her a few moments to understand his meaning.

"Are you saying we broke in? That you didn't ask the owner for permission for us to stay here?"

"No, *we* didn't break in. *I* merely bypassed the alarm system and picked the lock," he explained.

Jenna studied him carefully the entire time he spoke. If she didn't know better, she'd say he was enjoying himself.

"Do you even know the owner of this place?"

He looked properly hurt, which didn't affect her one bit.

"Of course I know him. Would I break into a stranger's cabin? I also know he doesn't use it this time of year." Riley gave her his most innocent expression. An expression Jenna knew from the past and didn't believe one bit.

Jenna sat up, wrapping the soft, warm quilt around her to keep out the chilly air.

She looked around the room and first noticed a fire crackling in the stone fireplace across the room. The furniture was rustic looking and obviously expensive. She had to assume the owner may call this rustic living, but it was still the ultimate in comfort.

"Just one of those mountain shacks, right?" she said wryly.

Riley half turned and reached behind him. He handed Jenna a fluffy fleece robe.

"Thank you." She shrugged it on as she climbed out of bed and tied its sash around her waist. She adjusted the collar so it stood up around her face. "Are you going to tell me who owns the cabin, or do I have to wait until the cops show up and arrest us for breaking and entering?"

"You have a smart mouth. Did you know that?"

"Thanks to you."

"I'm glad to see you know who to thank." He proceeded to kiss that mouth.

Jenna moaned softly as she looped her arms around his neck and pressed up against him. Her mouth opened against his loving assault, and her tongue danced with his. When his hand warmly caressed her breast, she whispered his name. He drew back slightly.

"I actually came up to tell you dinner is ready," he said thickly.

"Hmm? We can reheat it later," she murmured as her hand sneaked under his sweater. Her fingertips lightly rubbed his nipples. "I think they were right. The idea of danger is a wonderful aphrodisiac. Why don't we see how far we can get before the cops show up.''

Riley was very tempted. Jenna didn't need to even touch him for him to feel aroused. All he had to do was look at her.

"We both need to eat," he said, not sounding as calm as he should.

Jenna stepped back. The cat's smile on her lips told him she knew she affected him. "Give me ten minutes to freshen up.''

"I put your clothes in the closet.''

"Be careful, Riley, you're getting too domesticated,'' she teased.

After Riley left the room, Jenna headed for the closet.

She sorted through the clothing until she came to a dusty rose wool sweater and cream colored knit pants.

A quick shower along with fixing her hair and touch of makeup had her just barely making her self-imposed deadline.

Once downstairs she followed the homey aroma of beef stew. She found Riley seated at a butcher-block table with a bottle of beer set before him.

"And he cooks, too," she said lightly as she walked in. She walked over to the stove and lifted a pot lid. The contents sent her appetite soaring. She hadn't realized until then it had been more than twelve hours since she'd eaten a decent meal. "When did you learn to cook?''

"There aren't a lot of restaurants where I live, so if I wanted to eat more than what I could throw on a barbecue, I had to learn. Besides, stew isn't all that difficult. You throw a bunch of food in a pot and let it simmer.'' He pulled large, shallow bowls out of a cabinet and spoons from a drawer. ''Do you want a beer with your meal?''

Jenna shuddered. It was a taste she had never acquired. ''No, thank you. I'll see what else you have.'' She opened the refrigerator door and after inspecting the contents, pulled out a bottle of sparkling water flavored with orange. She chose a chair as Riley ladled out stew and dumplings. He set a bowl in front of each of them.

''Does the cabin belong to you?'' she asked, dipping her spoon into the stew. One taste told her Riley did know how to cook an excellent stew.

''Nope, but I assure you I do know the owner,'' Riley answered, digging into his food with relish.

She set her spoon down. ''Who owns the cabin, Riley? It can't be that much of a secret. Or am I going to be kept in the dark so I can't tell the police anything when they show up?''

Riley shook his head. ''The police won't show up,'' he assured her. ''And if it makes you feel better, the place belongs to my ex-boss, Mr. Benedict.''

Jenna's eyes widened. ''Are you saying he owns this cabin?''

''It's not as if he's on the take or something. He just has a wife with a hefty trust fund. They built this place more for their kids than themselves. The kids like coming up here during the summer, and they sometimes come out for the Christmas holidays. Luckily they leave a pretty filled freezer and pantry. We won't need to worry about food for some time.''

"Why didn't you call him and ask if we could borrow it? Why did we have to break in?" she asked.

"Benedict would understand. Besides, I did him a big favor. He really needs to see about getting a better security system."

Jenna set her spoon down. Her appetite had taken a pretty nasty nosedive. "From what I remember you saying about him he would not understand. Which means if you hadn't been able to bypass the alarm, the local law would have been out here and we'd be in more trouble than we are now."

Riley heaved a sigh. "I would have taken care of everything." He waved off her concerns. "I called Dave a little while ago, but he wasn't in. I'll try him again later," he said. "I didn't want to leave any kind of message on his voice mail. I'm hoping his being out means he was able to dig up something."

The rich aroma of her dinner weakened any further arguments she might have made.

"I refuse to worry any longer about the worst that can happen," she announced, picking up her spoon again. "From now on, mealtime will be a happy time. I refuse to have my appetite ruined with our worrying about someone carrying a submachine gun breaking in here at any moment."

"They'd more likely be carrying an Uzi or AK-47. I doubt it would happen that way." Riley got up and refilled his bowl along with snagging a second bottle of beer from the refrigerator. He sat down and ate several bites before looking up. "So, who do you think will win the Super Bowl this season?"

Riley shooed Jenna out of the kitchen after dinner, stating he'd prefer doing the cleanup by himself. She wasn't about to protest and announced she was going to explore their surroundings. When she found a nicely stocked library, she picked out some reading material. With a novel in hand, she returned upstairs with the intention of relaxing in a nice hot bath.

Jenna hadn't had a chance to check out the master bathroom earlier, so she took the opportunity now.

It only took one look to tell her the room was large enough to house a small family.

A huge step-down tub with faucets in the shape of swans was set in a corner with foliage all around for privacy.

"Why, Marshal Benedict, you sly dog you." She grinned, pulling a couple of fluffy lilac-colored towels out of the linen closet. "With a tub like this I just bet you and your wife can't wait until the kids are asleep."

She started the water running, then studied the assorted bath salts and bath oils in bottles on shelves over the tub. She chose one and poured the bath salts into the hot water.

Once the tub was full, Jenna shed her clothing and settled down into the water. She closed her eyes and sighed her bliss as she sank down until the water reached her neck as she rested the back of her head against a rolled up towel.

"Are you telling me you can't find one damned thing? What good is that fancy computer system if it doesn't tell you anything? And how come no one knew Grieco's business was down the tubes? How could something like that have gotten past anyone?"

Riley picked up the glass of scotch he'd poured earlier and downed it in one gulp. The explosion of heat in his stomach wasn't the least bit soothing, since stress was adding acid to the mixture. He never thought he'd get an ulcer. Now he was starting to change his mind about that possibility.

"As you said, it was all kept under wraps. Max checked it out thoroughly," Dave named his present partner. "He said it was definitely hush-hush because no one wanted a war. Pretty soon it didn't matter because the business wasn't worth a plugged nickel. Grieco's men didn't care when their boss went to prison, because they figured on fighting over the business. Instead, everyone lost."

"None of it makes sense," Riley argued. "What about John Smith's boss?"

"Smith is very good at what he does because we couldn't find his prints in the system," Dave told him. "He's a total unknown."

Riley switched the cordless phone to his other ear. "Great, so what you're saying is a ghost is looking to kill me."

"No, I'm just saying I looked through all your past cases and the name Smith gave you didn't come up. I also ran a check on the name through the computer and it didn't come up there either. He gave you a bogus name, which is probably what the man gave Smith. I guess the money was so good he hadn't bothered to check out his boss."

Riley swore long and hard. Dave waited patiently until he was through.

"Then he must be connected to one of my cases in another way," Riley said finally.

"Riley, his name doesn't come up in the computer," Dave argued.

"There has to be something there. Did you check every angle? No matter how insignificant?" Riley started to refill the glass then stopped. The last thing he needed right now was to blunt his senses. He dropped onto the closest chair and stretched his legs out in front of him.

"Hell, yes, I checked every angle! What do you take me for, Cooper? A rookie? I checked people out so thoroughly, on any given day I can tell you what color underwear they're wearing."

"Then check them again. I'll call you in the morning." He pressed the Talk button, effectively cutting off Dave's furious sputtering.

He tipped his head back and stared at the ceiling. He thought of Jenna in the room above.

He wanted a future with her.

For the past few years he hadn't thought beyond the next twenty-four hours. As far as he was concerned, he hadn't any reason to. Now it was different.

He wanted to think beyond the next twenty-four hours. He wanted to think about a long future with Jenna.

Jenna was content to drift in a twilight world of half sleep with the quiet all around her. She didn't find it jarring when the erotic sound of bluesy jazz wrapped itself around her. She opened her eyes and found Riley walking into the bathroom.

"If I'd known Benedict's cabin was this nice, I would have brought us up here first thing," he told her. "His sound system is hooked up to play throughout the entire house. I thought you might appreciate a little music with your bath.''

She kept her eyes at half mast as she watched him start to shed his clothing.

"I hope you don't mind some company. Damn!" he cursed as he stepped one foot into the water. "This is hot enough to peel skin."

"I added more hot water not long ago. It's relaxing." She shifted her body as he slowly submerged himself an inch at a time.

Riley shifted Jenna around until she rested against his chest.

"I shouldn't feel this relaxed," she said, her voice drowsy. "After all, a man wants to kill us. We've been on the run for weeks. All we've accomplished is my nearly getting killed and you probably wishing you'd stayed where you were." She turned her head to nestle her cheek against his collarbone.

Riley threaded his fingers through her hair, pushing it back from her face. His fingers then trailed down her throat, finding the vulnerable pulse point.

"You're in this mess because of me, Smitty," he said quietly, using his free hand to scoop up water and let it trickle out between his fingers. "I'm going to make it right."

"By making it right, you could get hurt in the process." She refused to use a stronger word for fear her saying it could make it come true.

"It happens. Hell, I could walk out onto a street tomorrow and get hit by a bus."

"You've taken your chances and you have the scars to prove it." She tried to twist around to face him, but he made sure she couldn't do so. "Let someone else take the chances this time. You told Dave you were taking me away to keep me safe. Fine, that's what you're doing. It's their job to do the rest."

"I'm not the same man you knew several years ago," he said quietly. "When I got out, I drank, I did whatever was necessary to drive you out of my mind. Except I couldn't do it. I'd swear I could smell your scent in my clothing or feel you against me while I slept. They say you can't run from your demons, and they're right.

"I'm giving up running. I don't want to lose you again. I want you always with me, Jenna. We've gone through the bad times and survived. I want us to think about looking for some good ones." His crooked smile told her of his uncertainty about how she'd react.

"I had to force myself not to draw your face," she confessed. "I didn't dare have a blank sheet of paper in front of me."

Riley's chest shook with his chuckle. "We're pretty pathetic, aren't we?"

"No, we're not. We followed the rules and we're together. Maybe it's a sign that we're meant to be." Jenna held her breath. He remained with her in a loose embrace.

He twisted around enough so she could see his face. "Are you asking me if you can wear my letterman's jacket?"

"What I'm saying is you aren't going to get rid of me that easily this time, either, Riley Cooper," she said firmly. She turned around so she was straddling his hips, then she circled his waist with her arms. "I'm no longer that delicate flower who has to be protected from the dark forces." She staunchly ignored his uplifted brow and the amusement written on his face. "All right, I did get a little crazy when John Smith grabbed me, but I hadn't expected it. I thought I was perfectly safe out there."

"Jen, you can't expect him to call ahead to let you know he was coming," Riley said with infinite patience.

She rolled her eyes. "You know very well what I mean. I won't break down again. I promise." Her dark eyes glimmered with purpose. "And I won't make it easy for anyone, either."

Riley leaned forward and brushed his lips across hers. "I know you won't." He eyed her breasts, which gleamed from the water streaming down them, the rosy tips taut in the cool air. "Although I hope you'll make me an exception?"

She rotated her hips against him. "I always did like a tough guy," she purred.

Riley may have been a tough guy, but he was gentle with Jenna as he brought her breast up to his mouth. He suckled on the nipple, drawing it deep into his mouth, curling his tongue around the taut peak.

Jenna grasped the back of his head as she arched against his heated touch. Needing to be closer, she twined her legs around his waist and pressed down onto him until they were joined. As she did so, she pulled his face up to hers for a deep probing kiss.

"Wait a minute," Riley muttered in a raw voice, moving to leave the tub.

Jenna grabbed his arm.

"No," she whispered. "I need to feel all of you, Riley. It's all right." She drew him back down to her.

Riley groaned as he felt her melt against him.

Water sloshed all around them, Riley held tight to Jenna's hips as he thrust deeply inside her. Her body contracted around him, pulling him in even deeper until he felt as if they were truly one. Nothing else mattered at that moment. If they were to die, so be it, but he would do all that was possible to keep them alive.

He was afraid their coming here might only have put her in more danger. But he didn't think they could take off again. They might not get that second chance he'd just talked about. Were they fated to run across the country one step ahead of a killer? He wouldn't allow them to be parted again. Not this time. But was there no choice in the matter? Would they be fated to only have memories of their time together?

Riley wouldn't need memories. At that moment, his soul had truly joined with hers.

Jenna's body was still quivering in aftershocks as she collapsed against him.

"Do you think we flooded the bathroom?" she murmured, rubbing her cheek against his chest. She idly combed her fingers through the damp hair matted against his skin.

"More likely we flooded the whole house." Needing to keep on touching her, he lazily stroked the long lines of her bare back. "Good thing there's plenty of towels in here." He eased her off him and stood up, then helped her up.

They both eyed the puddles of water streaming across the tile floor and started laughing.

Riley grabbed several towels and dropped them on the floor. He took another, wrapping it around Jenna before taking one for himself.

"You really know how to catch a guy's attention," he said.

Jenna picked up another towel. She bent over and wrapped it around her wet hair. She eyed him askance as she tucked the towel into itself.

"If I recall correctly, I was having a nice leisurely bath when you decided to come in and take over the tub."

"I didn't hear any arguments on your part."

She smiled. "How could I, when you looked so cute sitting among all those bubbles." Her smile suddenly turned wobbly. "I'm scared, Riley."

Her whispered last words sent pain shooting through his heart. He immediately gathered her into his arms.

"Go ahead, baby, let it out," he whispered, holding her tightly.

Jenna cried. She cried for what they'd had in the beginning. She cried for the day she had left him behind. She cried for what brought him back into her life, and she cried for what they had gained and could still lose.

In between sobs she told him everything she felt. She told him how much she loved him. How she missed him all this time and she didn't care if she was selfish, she didn't want to give him up again.

"I know you don't want children," she sobbed as she lay in his arms. "I just want to be with you,

Riley. All those years, I couldn't have stopped loving you if I tried. It would have been as if I tried to stop breathing. I'm so afraid someone will try to separate us again. I don't want that to happen.''

Riley listened to her words, feeling the same pain.

Should he tell her that he was afraid, too? Afraid that they should have left Mexico sooner. Afraid that no matter what precautions he took, there was a chance someone else would find them. Afraid that the next time they wouldn't be so lucky.

Jenna deserved to be safe. After what happened, he didn't trust the Witness Relocation Program. Not that it wasn't excellent. For now he just didn't feel it was right for Jenna.

His own life didn't matter. He was going to do whatever was necessary to make Jenna safe. He wanted her to laugh again and he wanted her to find a way to paint again.

He framed her face with his hands.

Her eyes were red rimmed and wet with tears. Even her nose was red at the tip, and her lower lip quivered. She wore no makeup.

''You are so beautiful that I ache when I look at you,'' he whispered.

If Jenna sensed he was telling her more, she didn't show it. Her facial muscles twitched slightly before she smiled. ''And it's because you say lovely things like that, that I love you so much.''

She was still smiling when he picked her up and carried her into the bedroom.

When Jenna awoke she was alone in the bed.

Her senses told her that Riley was gone. Not just

from her bed, but from the room.

She rolled over, pulling his pillow toward her. She could still smell his scent on the fine cotton.

She got out of bed and pulled on her robe, then went downstairs and headed for the kitchen.

When she stepped inside, she found Riley seated at the table. He was reading a newspaper and had a cup of coffee in front of him. He stood up when she entered.

"Don't tell me we even have our very own paperboy all the way out here?" she said dryly.

"Actually, it's from last summer." He held it up so she could see the date on the first page. "I had no idea this area boasted such a wild life. They have a Fourth of July parade and carnival and everything. I'm really jealous Benedict never invited me out here."

"He obviously knew better." Jenna waved him to sit back down and started for the coffeepot. She poured herself a cup and sat down.

"Want some breakfast?" he asked. "I make a pretty good omelette."

"I'd like that. But there's something else I want you to do," she said softly.

Riley raised an eyebrow. "Why, Smitty, I'm shocked. In the kitchen?" He looked around the room. "I guess the table would be the most comfortable."

She gave him her "I'm being serious here" look. "Not this time, handsome. No, I want you to teach me how to shoot. I don't want to take any chances."

Chapter 14

"Do you know what time it is?" Dave snarled.

Riley tucked the phone between his shoulder and ear. "This is important."

"You're calling me here at three-freaking-o'clock in the morning because you think something is important? I don't think so." Dave lowered his voice. "Look, if Kate doesn't get her full eight hours, she's really grumpy in the morning."

"Blame it on me." Riley walked back and forth as if the motion helped him think better. "I want to go through the files, but I need a password."

"You called to get my password? You couldn't call at a normal time?"

"I got the idea now. I figured I'd call now. I thought I might see if something might jump out at me that you might not have noticed."

Dave sighed. "Pywacket."

"Pywacket?" Riley hooted. "Really?"

"I always thought Kim Novak in *Bell, Book and Candle* was one hot lady. Is there anything else you require? A computer, perhaps?"

"No, thanks, I have that part covered. I'll let you know if I find anything." Riley hung up.

Within moments he was using Benedict's computer and was in the data system he required. Riley lost track of time as he scanned one file after another. He had no idea what time it was when he absently noticed a cup of steaming coffee set in front of him. As he worked, he picked it up to drink every so often. When he emptied it, it was filled again.

"So what are you looking for?" Jenna asked. She'd taken possession of a nearby chair and sat curled up in the soft depths. She held a mug filled with hot chocolate in her hands.

"I'm not really sure. But I'll know when I find it." Riley squinted at the screen.

"You shouldn't be staring so close to the screen. Maybe you need reading glasses."

"No, I don't need reading glasses," he said grumpily. Tapping a few keys, he paused, read what was on the screen then tapped a few more keys. At one point he sat back and just stared at the screen. "Why isn't there anything in the files on Martin Randolph?" he murmured to himself.

"Who's Martin Randolph?" Jenna asked.

"The nephew of a man who was executed about four years ago. Martin supposedly died in a car accident in Germany not long after that. All through the trial he was adamant his uncle, Leonard Randolph, was innocent. The evidence said otherwise," he murmured. "When Leonard escaped from prison, I was brought in to bring him back. Before I could catch up with the bastard, he raped, tortured and murdered four teenage girls. Once captured, he was tried again and sentenced to death. Needless to say, old Leonard's family weren't too fond of me for bringing him back. They all stood up in court and claimed Leonard had emotional problems and needed help. The court and the psychiatrists disagreed."

Lost in thought, Riley rocked back and forth in the chair.

"You don't think he's dead, do you?" Jenna asked, easily catching on to his line of thought.

He clasped his hands behind his head as shrugged. "My gut tells me he's not. He wouldn't be the first person to fake his own death, and his family had already washed their hands clean of him. It's common knowledge if you have enough money you can get yourself a new identity with little problem. He had the money for it and with his 'death' happening in Europe, there's no reason for anyone to think otherwise. The Randolph family was worth millions, so he had the financial resources. In his mind, he had a pretty good reason for hating me. I guess he and his uncle were pretty close." He shook his head at the idea of someone carrying that heavy a load of hate.

He straightened up and shut down the computer. He turned to Jenna. "Time for some fresh air and shooting lessons for you."

Jenna smiled as if he'd just granted her most heartfelt wish. She glanced down at the sweater and leggings she wore. "I'll go change." She pushed herself off her chair and ran upstairs.

* * *

Jenna lay on the ground. She was positive that every bone in her body was broken.

She ignored the outstretched hand for a moment. She told herself she would need his help to get to her feet.

"Is there a reason why we couldn't have practiced these moves on a softer surface?" she groused, rubbing her bruised posterior.

"There's no guarantee you'll be defending yourself where there's a thick carpet," he told her.

"I don't intend on falling," she stated with a stubborn tilt to her chin.

"More power to you if you don't."

"Why do we have to do it out here?" she asked, fearing there might be a slight whine in her voice. "It's cold, and the ground is so hard."

Riley noticed the blue tint to her lips and took pity.

"Okay. Let's take the next hour to practice your shooting, then we'll use the workout room." He turned and headed for the house.

"Workout room? You mean there's a workout room in there that's heated?" she shrieked, rounding on him with fists.

Riley laughed and picked her up, tossing her over his shoulder. "Trust me, it's better for you working out here."

"Balance. You have to keep your balance!" Riley shouted as he held a punching bag he had Jenna use for practice kicks. "If you don't, you'll end up on your butt and be a prime target."

She spun in a tight circle, then lashed out with her foot. Riley grunted as the bag slammed into his body.

"Good. Very good."

She lifted her hand in reply, then she half bent over with her hands resting on her knees.

Picking up her water bottle, Riley walked over and handed it to her. She grasped it tightly and seemed to inhale half the contents.

"I thought I was supposed to defend myself, not kill myself!" she wheezed.

"If you had known how to defend yourself earlier that sleaze wouldn't have been able to get the better of you. That's why I taught you to use your nails, your elbows, feet and knees. If someone tries to go after you, I want you to fight back with no holds barred."

Jenna picked up a towel and mopped her face. It didn't matter, since she could feel sweat pouring down her body. She'd pulled her hair back, but it was also matted and wet from her exertion.

For the past three days Riley had been a tyrant in teaching her to shoot and renewing their self-defense lessons.

He bullied her into a five-mile run every morning then spent two hours teaching her how to handle a weapon. In the afternoons he had her practice self-defense and a smattering of kickboxing.

All Jenna knew was that this hard regimen was wearing her out. Each night she collapsed in bed positive every muscle in her body ached. She murmured curses at Riley as he chuckled and curved his body around hers.

* * *

Jenna was grateful when Riley started spending extra hours at the computer. That meant he wasn't trying to turn her entire body black-and-blue. Not to mention her ears ringing from the sound of the shots as she practiced hitting cans and bottles.

She just didn't expect he had other plans for her. One morning she woke up and found a box by the bed. Riley, who had appeared with two mugs of coffee, grinned at her.

"I've been waiting for the right moment to give this to you. I guess this is as good a time as any." He set the mugs on the nightstand and reached down for the box.

Jenna looked uncertain as she studied the box. There was nothing written on the sides to give her a hint as to its contents. She looked up at Riley, but he merely smiled.

"Open it," he urged her.

She pulled back the flaps and bent them back. She looked inside and stared at the contents without saying a word.

"Since you're not jumping up and down with joy or covering me with kisses, I guess it isn't what you expected." Riley watched her without any expression on his face.

Jenna slowly reached into the box and pulled out sketch pads, drawing pencils and a variety of paints. She didn't look at him as she carefully set each item on the bed.

"Why did you get these?" she asked quietly. "And when?"

"I got them while you were buying your clothes for the colder weather. And I got them because you need to practice your painting again. There's plenty of scenery around here for you to paint all you want.''

Jenna quickly returned them to the box and closed it back up. "I don't paint anymore."

Riley's fists were on his hips. He looked off in the distance for a moment as if seeking the right words before turning back to her. ''Painting is part of your soul. You can't just stop doing what you've always loved.''

''Yes, I can. I taught myself that it can no longer be in my life, and I've done just fine without it,'' she said stubbornly.

The staring contest was on, and it didn't take long to see neither was going to give up.

''Damn, you were never this stubborn before,'' Riley said, still refusing to blink.

Jenna didn't say a word. She moved the box to one side and climbed out of bed.

She headed for the bathroom with her coffee mug in hand. As she reached the doorway, she turned around. Her eyes glistened with tears.

''The doctor said I'd probably have trouble writing my name from now on,'' she whispered. ''If I can't even write my name how can you think I could draw a simple straight line?'' She turned back, went into the bathroom and closed the door after her.

''Sweetheart, you can do anything you want. You just need to tell yourself that,'' he murmured.

When Jenna finally ventured out of the bathroom she found Riley and the box gone. She thought the subject was finished. She should have known better.

* * *

Jenna had a quiet breakfast, while Riley closeted himself in the office. She thought of calling him a few choice names when she found a sketch pad and drawing pencils on the counter by the coffeepot. Instead she ignored their allure and fixed herself a quick breakfast. After she finished cleaning the kitchen, she carried two mugs of coffee into the office.

Riley was seated at the desk, staring at the computer monitor as if it would give him all the right answers.

Jenna set one of the mugs on the desk. She started to sit in her usual spot when she noticed the sketch pad and pencils lying on the seat. She shot him a knowing look and moved them to a nearby table.

As the morning passed, Jenna found herself looking out the floor-to-ceiling windows more and more. She could see the blue-gray surface of the lake with the stark lines of the trees dotting the edge. The longer she looked outside, the more her imagination took flight.

Old habits took over as she absently reached for the sketch pad and pencils. She looked at the scene before her and began drawing without thinking twice.

Riley could see Jenna's reflection in the monitor. He watched her look out, then saw her head go down. Her movements were jerky, uncoordinated. Nothing like the smooth and graceful strokes he remembered from before. He could also see the raw determination etched on her face and her lips forming silent curses.

As he worked at the computer, he also kept one eye on her as she worked. He could see when frustration took over and listened to more than one pencil snap. But she never gave up. He knew if he said one word she would undoubtedly throw the pad and pencils at him. He remained silent and kept at his work.

It still didn't stop his daydreams. He wondered what she'd think if he told her he could visualize her sitting on the beach outside his beach shack. Sitting there and drawing the little Rileys running around. He'd teach them to surf. She'd teach them to draw.

He wasn't sure why he was thinking of them as the all-American couple raising the all-American kids. It had never been his style before. Of course, he hadn't reckoned on Jenna either. One thing she had proven to be was one tough cookie. If nothing else, he had to love her for that. With Jenna, he could see himself taking on the world and winning.

And every night he would go to sleep holding her in his arms. His idea of heaven.

Until then he had a job to do, and he intended to get it settled.

"If you wanted to change your identity, but make it something easy for you to remember what would you use for a name?" he suddenly spoke up.

Jenna looked up. "The name of a relative—mother's or grandmother's maiden name," she said. "Maybe even a close relative's middle name."

Riley snapped his fingers. He tapped a few keys. "Leonard Randolph's middle name was Carter, which was his mother's maiden name. Like I said, they were old money." He kept on typing. "And there's a Carter Leonard. Age is right." He tapped a few more keys and a photo appeared on the screen. "Hair color and style isn't and eye color isn't, but that's easy enough to change. Facial structure isn't totally the same, but that's why plastic surgeons make the big bucks," he said to himself.

Jenna looked more alert. "Do you think he's the one behind all this?"

"Hard to say, but it's worth a try. He's living in Connecticut. He's the head of a financial consortium which really says very little. That kind of occupation could hide any number of activities," Riley said, reading off the screen. "He supposedly lived in Switzerland until four years ago. He arrived in New York, set up an office on Wall Street. Two years later, after amassing a notable fortune, he moved to Connecticut and set up some sort of office compound there. Financial experts from all over the world visit him there."

Jenna got up from her chair and walked over to the desk. She looked over Riley's shoulder, reading the words on the screen.

"Why does he keep to himself?" Riley murmured, still scrolling downward and reading. "And why does he employ such a large number of bodyguards? And have such a sophisticated security system unless he wants to keep people out?" He reached for the phone. Within moments he was connected to Dave and telling him everything he'd found. When he hung up, he was grinning from ear to ear.

"You honestly think you have the right person," Jenna said. There was nothing in her voice to indicate how she felt about that idea.

Riley nodded. He slid back his chair and stood up. In a swift movement, he picked her up and hugged her tightly.

"I feel it, Smitty. Dave will do even more digging

and there's going to be enough found to implicate the bastard.'' He swung her around in a circle.

Jenna looked as if she was afraid to hope it would soon be all over. The broad grin on Riley's face said otherwise.

His eyes danced as he kept hold of her.

Jenna arched an eyebrow. ''Riley Cooper, you have that look in your eye. You don't even know you're right.''

He started nuzzling the tender spot just behind her ear. ''I'm right,'' he muttered. ''Maybe they'll say they can't positively prove that Carter Leonard is really Leonard Randolph. But fingerprints don't lie. All they need is a strong enough lead and they can take it from there.''

Jenna clung to him. She wasn't sure whether to laugh with relief that it could all be over or cry for the same reason. ''Let's go outside for a walk.'' She shook her head at his bemused expression. ''I want to go outside without feeling I have to look over my shoulder all the time. I want to go outside feeling deep inside I'm truly Jenna Welles again.''

Riley smiled. ''I'll get our coats.''

Within moments they were walking along the shoreline with one of Jenna's hands snugly tucked into Riley's jacket pocket.

''You are a very sneaky man, Riley Cooper,'' she accused.

He was surprised. ''I've been called a lot of things, but sneaky is a new one.''

She stopped and turned to face him. ''You deliberately left drawing equipment in just about every room. You were trying to wear me down.''

He looked all too smug. "Looks like it worked, too."

She looked down at her gloved hand and thought of the pain whenever she attempted to hold the pencil. She knew she would have the same trouble when she started picking up brushes.

"Physical therapy will help with that," he said quietly, easily reading her mind. "You'll be able to start pretty soon too."

Jenna smiled at his determination, but it didn't quite reach her eyes.

"It wasn't easy to track him down, Riley. Do you honestly think he'll make it easy to be charged with what he did?"

"Nothing's easy, but this will be settled. No more running for either one of us."

"No more running," she repeated. "I'd like that."

The office was as cold as a cave and just as dark. The small lamp on the desk shed little light beyond the desk's bare surface.

"I do not like to hear that the man who came so highly recommended has now disappeared," the man behind the desk said in a voice as cold as his office.

The man standing before him—he was not invited to sit down—took a deep breath before replying.

"I've sent out queries, and it's as if he disappeared off the face of the earth, sir," he said in a quietly respectful tone that was not echoed inside him. He hated the man with a passion, but he knew better than to show his feelings. "Nothing has been heard from him since he arrived in Mexico."

The other man lit a cigar, the glow from the tip looking eerily like a devil's eye.

"I pay my people excellent wages because I expect a job well done. It appears this is something I will have to take care of myself." His smile was as dead as the expression in his eyes. "I want to know where they are, and I want to know by tomorrow morning. Do I make myself clear?"

"Yes, sir." He backed out of the dark office and hurried down the hallway. He silently cursed John Smith for putting him in this bind, and at the same time he silently cheered him for having found a way to escape.

"I don't want to do this anymore," Jenna panted. She dropped to the ground and flopped onto her back. The ground was hard with frost, but she was past caring. She was too tired to move.

Riley stood over her, his face glowing from the run they'd just finished. He didn't seem to have any problem catching his breath, she grumpily noticed. She knew if she had enough energy left she'd hurt him.

He'd hauled her out of bed at dawn for a run and today had even picked up the pace. Now she was so tired she didn't want to move from her hard resting place. Jenna felt ready to crawl into bed and stay there for a year.

"Ah, come on. You know you feel better for it," he told her.

She looked up at him with murder in her eyes. "I'd only feel better if you would drop with fatigue."

"Want to try some more kickboxing after lunch?"

Jenna gave a less-than-feminine snarl as she slowly sat up. "Only if you promise to stand very still. Better yet. Let me practice my shooting while you pretend to be the target."

Riley tsked and shook his head. "Don't be a grump. You wanted to do this."

"You just didn't have to enjoy torturing me so much." Jenna wrapped her arms around her drawn-up knees and rested her chin on them. "What if we could draw him out?"

Riley dropped to the ground beside her. "Are you saying what I think you're saying?"

She nodded. "Isn't that what you do when you want to catch someone who's hiding? Bait the trap with something they can't resist? Wouldn't he be ecstatic to get both of us?"

"No way," he said without hesitation.

"Why not?" she asked, starting to get huffy.

His jaw looked as if it had been carved out of granite. "Because this is my problem."

Jenna looked at him as if she couldn't believe what she was hearing.

"*Your* problem," she said slowly, "became *our* problem the night I was attacked. No arguments, Cooper. I'm in this just as much as you are."

"No, you're not. This man would kill you without a second thought just because he would want to do it." He held up his hand to silence her expected retort. "Just because you've learned some self-defense doesn't mean you're capable of protecting yourself against a trained killer. And that's what we're dealing with."

Jenna glared at him as she rose to her feet. She didn't say another word as she stalked into the house.

Even a long, hot shower didn't ease her temper any.

But she did find something that did calm her down.

She dragged out one of the sketch pads and several drawing pencils.

Her first strokes of the pencil were still awkward. But she didn't stop. Jenna was back for good.

Riley stayed out of Jenna's way for the rest of the afternoon. He figured it was safer that way. He called Dave and spent a couple hours on the phone, listening to what Dave had to say.

"I'd say you've found your man," Dave said, confirming his suspicions. "He's got quite a compound out there. It's got an electric gate and a block wall with broken glass and razor wire all across the top. He also has motion-detector lights all around the house and dogs that run loose all night. The closest house is ten miles away, and the closest town fifteen miles away. He obviously doesn't have drop-in company too often."

Riley clenched his fist and thrust it up in the air for victory. "Man, I'd love to be there when you go after the bastard."

"You forgot something, old buddy. Such as hard evidence. And I don't think that's something he leaves around on top of his desk. We did find out something interesting though." His voice grew quiet. "His personal jet is having some mechanical work done and he was insistent it be ready for takeoff by tomorrow morning. The flight plan was filed for Denver.''

Riley grew still. "There's no way he could have tracked us here.''

"If you get Benedict's place shot up, he's going to be really ticked off," Dave said with dark humor. "He's already having a fit because you broke in there so easily. He was positive the place was locked up as tight as Fort Knox."

Riley winced. He had been more than familiar with his former superior's infamous temper.

"Just goes to show he needs to reevaluate his alarm system. Just reassure him we haven't had any orgies." He switched the phone from one ear to the other. "Yet."

He could hear Dave's heavy sigh. "I suppose you figured out the combination to his gun safe, too."

"Piece of cake." He walked back and forth, too antsy to stand still. Besides, he always felt he did his best thinking when he was moving. He took a deep breath. "I need you to come out here and get her. Hopefully, before they show up."

Riley looked down and saw the sketch pad lying on a table. He used his fingertip to lift the top and flip it back. He did that with several pages. True, they didn't show the grace of the work he remembered, but he saw something else there. The stark lines and slashes were those of a woman who'd grown far beyond the person she had been.

He swallowed the lump in his throat as he moved on to find a sketch of himself. He looked hard and dangerous, due to the strong strokes of the pencil.

Just the way he'd felt lately. Except for the time he spent with her.

"Riley?" From the sound of Dave's voice he'd said the name more than once.

"Ya," he murmured, "I'm here."

Riley was determined to finish this. He wasn't going to allow Jenna to be afraid any longer.

Chapter 15

"**I**s it safe?"

Jenna looked up from her drawing. Riley stood in the doorway holding up a white handkerchief in one hand. The other was hidden behind his back. She tried not to smile at his sign of surrender, but her lips twitched, anyway.

"Safe enough," she said, closing her sketch pad and setting it to one side. "Where have you been hiding?"

He walked into the room, holding out his other arm, revealing a bottle of wine and two glasses.

"Here and there. Mostly there, figuring out the combination to Benedict's wine closet. He used his and his wife's birth dates. Not a good idea. He may be a great lawman, but he has no imagination."

Jenna was sitting cross-legged in the middle of the bed with her black-and-red flannel patchwork skirt billowed around her. She had pushed up the sleeves to her black knit top.

Riley set the glasses down and poured wine into them.

"What's the celebration for?" she asked.

"We figured out who's behind this. Dave's happy. We're happy. That's all that's needed."

Jenna uttered a short laugh of relief.

"Do you mean it's over? We can go home?"

Riley's heart ached at the sound of joy in her voice. He should tell her the truth, but she'd hate him for it. No, better to have this all-too-short celebration. She could hate him later. For now, he wanted to share in her exhilaration.

Instead he picked up one of the wineglasses and dipped his finger into the contents. He then proceeded to paint her lips with the wine. Once they were wet and glistening, he leaned forward and delicately licked the moisture from them. She smiled as he repeated the gesture.

Jenna dipped her fingertip in the glass and did the same thing to Riley. Then she dipped her finger in again and this time traced a line down his throat. She unbuttoned his flannel shirt, her finger still trailing downward. As her tongue followed the path, she pulled his shirt out of his jeans, then unfastened them.

"Smitty." His voice was ragged with desire as he watched her pull his jeans downward.

She looked up with a smile that turned her eyes a dazzling blue. She took the wineglass out of his hand and spilled droplets onto his bare chest.

"Just lie back and relax, Riley," she murmured in

a husky voice guaranteed to send shivers along his spine.

"Relax? I'll be lucky if I don't die within the next ten seconds," he said in a strangled voice.

"I want you alive, Cooper." She lapped up the wine with a feline grace, and followed the droplets farther down.

Riley wanted to close his eyes against the exquisite pain Jenna was inflicting. But he couldn't stop watching her love him so passionately. It could have been minutes, it could have been hours. All he knew was he would die among the stars.

Unable to take anymore, he grabbed her arms and pulled her up over him. Her skirt billowed around him as she settled down upon him. He hissed what could have been a curse or a prayer as he discovered she wore no underwear and was hot and wet.

He arched upward, thrusting deep inside her. At the same time Jenna lowered her face to his, kissing him deeply, her tongue teasing him as her body teased his.

Riley's eyes were like polished stones as he watched the woman he had claimed so long ago and intended to keep beyond forever. Her eyes glittered with raw desire as she looked down at him.

"No more looking over our shoulders, Riley," she whispered as she moved her hips in a manner that had him groaning her name. "No more worries. I won't go back to what I was, and I won't let you leave me. You're stuck with me."

"We're stuck with each other," he whispered back, wanting to accelerate the rhythm but wanting their loving to last forever.

In the end there was no way they could prolong it. Jenna's breathing hitched a note as she moved her hips faster. Riley held on to her, watching her lose herself just before he couldn't hold back any longer and followed her into the star-filled void.

Jenna lay against his chest. Her body quivered with aftershocks.

Riley licked his lips. For a moment he wasn't sure if he could form a coherent word.

"I think we could get a hell of a lot better once we get some practice in."

Jenna laughed. She lifted her head and kissed him. "You were the one who started this."

"Maybe so, but then you took over and just about killed me." He brushed her hair from her face, his hands warmly cupping her cheeks. "I could never get tired of looking at your face," he murmured.

She blinked rapidly. "Don't say things that will make me cry."

Something—his conscience, maybe—tugged deep inside. She had no idea what was going to happen. What he had planned for her. She would probably hate him afterward, and he couldn't blame her. She wouldn't understand that he was doing it for a good reason. She would hate him with equal good reason.

When it was all over, he would just have to do whatever was necessary to make her love him again.

"I promise, I will never make you cry unless it's for a good reason."

Jenna looked uncertain for a moment then smiled again. "As long as it's for a good reason."

Riley wrapped his arms around her and allowed sleep to overtake him even as he sensed her also falling asleep. He knew as long as he held on to her, nothing could hurt them.

Jenna wasn't sure what woke her up. It was as if something unwanted had shifted the air in the house.

She sat up carefully in hopes she wouldn't awaken Riley and remained very still. She let her senses reach out as she waited for her eyes to adjust to the darkness. Except she now knew what woke her wasn't something she needed to see, but something she could hear. The soft hiss of helicopter blades.

She looked down and saw Riley's eyes open.

"They couldn't have found us," she said more in hopes he'd agree with her. But there was no smile or words of reassurance. Just an expression of sad acceptance.

Riley straightened up and got off the bed. He snatched up his clothing and pulled it on.

Jenna stood by the bed and silently watched him dress. It wasn't until he picked up her sketch pad and pencils, putting them in a tote bag that she realized the significance of his actions.

She ran to the window and looked out. There was no doubt the helicopter parked a short distance away had a the seal of the U.S. Marshal's Service on it. She spun around.

"Is there anything else you want to take with you?" Riley asked quietly.

Jenna said nothing. She went over to the closet, gathered up clothing and escaped to the bathroom.

Even over the thunder of the shower, Riley could hear her crying and cursing his name. He moved like a tired old man as he packed the rest of her clothing.

When Jenna walked out of the bathroom, her eyes were dry and red. She didn't say a word as she followed him out of the house to the waiting helicopter. As they approached it, the door swung open and Dave stepped out. He looked at one and then the other.

Jenna looked at him for one long moment, then turned to Riley. The pain in her eyes was as sharp as a laser.

"You trained me to take care of myself." Her anger fairly flew from her mouth. "You can't just make me leave without a fight."

"Are you sure?" Dave asked from behind Jenna.

Riley took a deep breath. He glanced over her shoulder.

"She's going with you, Dave."

His words were enough to unleash the final torrent.

"I won't be your pawn any longer!" she shouted, her fists clenched at her sides. For a moment Riley was positive she was going let go and hit him.

"You just can't stop pushing me away when things get rough, can you?" she screamed. "It's easier for you to let me go than to stick to something!"

She shook off Dave's restraining hand. But he persevered and grabbed her arm, gently pulling her back toward the helicopter. She dug in her heels, but he was stronger.

Riley stood there, not reacting to the anguish marring her face or the harsh tears rolling down her cheeks. He didn't flinch as the blades started rotating and the roar of the engine assaulted his eardrums. And he didn't turn away as the helicopter slowly lifted and all he could see was Jenna's face pressed against the glass.

It was clear at that moment that she realized exactly why he was sending her away.

"I kept my promise, Smitty. I wasn't going to make you cry unless it was for a good reason."

Riley worked tirelessly all afternoon. Thanks to a knack with electronics, he was able to set up a few surprises for any unwanted visitors. He emptied Benedict's gun safe and hid a gun in every room he could, and a few outside. He used pots and pans to booby-trap the kitchen, and he kept all the lights off so he would be accustomed to the dark once night fell.

When he finished that, he went upstairs and threw on a pair of black jeans and a black sweatshirt.

He had a feeling his enemy would prefer to swoop down on him in the middle of the night. He intended to be ready.

Hours passed as he sat in the middle of the bed. Here he was surrounded by Jenna's scent. His ears pricked up when he heard the faint roar of an outboard engine. Then it abruptly cut off. He rose from his position and stuck his handgun in the back of his jeans.

Stealthily he made his way down the stairs and waited near the front door. The slight crunch of hard-packed snow breaking under heavy feet was enough warning to keep him on alert. He couldn't see anything because there was no moon, but he figured there was only one person out there. If he was lucky, it was the man who was behind the terrorism. He remained in a dark corner, waiting.

It only took long enough for the front door to explode into splintered wood for Riley to realize he'd underestimated his opponent.

The smoke and flying wood made a distraction that could have killed him if he hadn't been fast on his feet.

"Dammit, who said he could have a nightscope," he muttered, running for the rear of the house. Several shots rang over his head and another hit a wall just a second before he did.

Riley ran for the kitchen hoping to gain some time as he headed for the rear door. The sound of metal hitting the floor and a man's fluent curses told him he had the advantage. For now.

As he raced outside, he knew his dark clothing would stand out against the light snow on the ground, so he could only hope to be faster.

He slipped and slid on the icy ground, falling to his hands several times. Each time he immediately pushed himself up and continued running.

"You can't go far, Cooper," a man's voice rang out. "Come on back before you turn into a Popsicle."

He didn't answer, and he didn't stop. After all, he wanted his attacker to follow him down a path he'd already charted.

Riley wasn't worried when he reached a pile of rocks. He knew there were two weapons close at hand along with the one he still carried. He stood back among the rocks to frustrate his opponent, more than anything.

Riley's enemy appeared in the clearing. The rifle he held with familiarity had a nightscope, and Riley already knew the ammunition he used in it was illegal.

"You've run an excellent game, Cooper," he called out, turning his head right and left, scanning the area for anything that moved. "I congratulate you on evading my man so easily. But the game is over. And once I finish here, you will have died with the knowledge I will be leaving here so I can dispense with your woman." He laughed. "I told you before all you need is enough money and anything can be accomplished."

Riley stepped out of the shadows. He wasn't afraid of the man shooting him point-blank. Now he knew for sure who his adversary was. This man wanted Riley dead. But first he meant to toy with him the way a cat toys with a mouse before pouncing.

"I don't know, Carter," he said, displaying a nonchalance he knew would irritate the man. "You paid that other guy some big bucks, I'm sure, and all he ended up with was a bullet for his trouble."

Even in the dark, Riley could see the other man's chilling smile.

"Which is why I'm here to finish the job." He started to lift the rifle. "I only wish I could make you suffer the way my uncle suffered. I promised my family I would do whatever was necessary to escort you out of this lifetime. Don't bother praying, Cooper. There's no one to hear you."

Riley didn't waste any time making his move. The moment the rifle was swung upward, he dove down and slid across the hard ground, tackling him at the knees. As the man lost his balance, the rifle went flying. Carter tried to reach for the weapon tucked against Riley's back, but Riley rolled over just in time. It didn't stop him from knotting his fists together and bringing them down hard on Riley's head.

Riley fell back, but quickly regained his balance. He swore his ears were ringing, but it didn't stop him from going after the man as Carter frantically searched for his rifle. Before he reached it, he first tried to hit Riley. Instead of hitting him square in the face, Riley veered away and received the blow along his cheek. He blinked and shook his head to clear it and dove again for the man.

Riley knew his only chance was to reach one of the guns before Carter grabbed his rifle. He grunted as a tree branch connected with his midsection but he still had enough power to hit the man in the face hard enough to force him to step back.

Riley then reached for the rifle and was ready to make a run for it when Carter reached for it, too. It looked as if Carter would reach it first when a shot rang out.

Carter spun around, surprise written on his face as he staggered past Riley. The smile on his face wasn't pleasant. Neither was the red blossom staining his shoulder.

"You won't win!" Jenna shouted from the cover of trees.

"Yes, I will," Carter declared as he reached for his rifle.

Riley leaped for it at the same time. His fingers scrambled for the trigger just as Carter's did. The shot seemed to boom in the silence. He spun around and stared at Riley for long seconds.

"My family will be very disappointed," he said just before dropping to the ground.

Riley fell back as every ounce of adrenaline left his body. He looked through his one good eye at the woman standing about six feet from him. She held a handgun that was now pointed at the ground.

"I do hope you were aiming at him and not me," he said just before the darkness took him.

"You are such a fool. I swear, Riley, if you die, I will never forgive you."

Riley felt as if he was wrapped in black cotton batting that was better than any bed, but the voice wouldn't leave him alone. He heard words of love and prayers. A distant part of his brain told him it was time to open his eyes.

The minute he did, he wished he hadn't because that's when the pain made itself known with a wallop.

Jenna was curled up asleep in a hard chair, her head cradled on her crossed arms resting on the chair arm.

"Hey, Smitty," he croaked.

Her eyes flew open, and she swiftly moved over to his bedside. "It's about time you woke up, you faker," she whispered.

He looked past her at the chair. "Wouldn't they let you curl up here with me?"

Jenna gestured to the medical equipment and the many lines, most of them attached to him. "Not unless you wanted me to set off a variety of alarms."

He licked his lips, finding them dry and cracked. "How long have I been out?"

"Three days. You have a concussion, a broken cheekbone, two broken ribs, a black eye and a variety of cuts and scrapes." She picked up the hand that didn't have an IV tube hooked into it and placed it against her cheek. "You sent me away because you knew he'd come, didn't you?"

He tried to laugh only to groan when pain shot through his chest. He reminded himself not to do that again.

"Yeah, I knew."

"And what if he had killed you?"

That was something he didn't want to think about.

"Dave knew what to do. Speaking of Dave, how did you get back there?"

Jenna smiled. "After we landed, he escorted me to a hotel where he'd booked a suite. As soon as I could, I locked him in the extra room and took off. I found someone to take me across the lake. When I saw the boat at the dock, I knew you were in trouble and I snuck into the house first. Luckily I found a gun, and I followed the sounds." She shook her head, trying to erase the picture that had haunted her since that night. "If he had killed you, I wouldn't want him to live."

"You wouldn't have wanted his death on your conscience, love. Don't worry. You slowed him down. I finished the job." He tried to smile and found out that hurt, too. "You did fine, love. You did fine."

"Fine? You weren't the one locked up." Dave strolled in carrying a balloon bouquet. More than one sported a risqué saying. "What can I say? You know how twisted the office is." He looked Riley over. "You look like a steamroller went over you a few times."

"Which is just the way I feel." Riley tried to sit up and discovered that was another bad idea. "What about Carter?"

Jenna and Dave exchanged looks.

"Your bullet found its way into his black heart. A couple of marshals went out to talk to his family. They had wanted vengeance because they thought Leonard Randolph had always been innocent. After he escaped and killed a few more, they realized there was no hope for him, but they kept it quiet. Only the nephew wanted you dead. They figured all the bad publicity wouldn't help the family holdings, so they were more than willing to write the guy off."

Riley looked at Jenna then gave Dave a pointed look.

He threw up his hands. "I'm outta here." He headed for the door. "So, you planning to return to us? Benedict would like nothing more than to have you back under his thumb for a while. You know, I never knew the man could cry until he toured his house. It was one pitiful sight, let me tell you. He kept muttering something about finding you the dirtiest duty he could."

"Tell him he won't have to worry about seeing me in this lifetime," Riley vowed. He turned back to Jenna. "I've got this shack on the beach," he said slowly. "It's not much and may take more than a little fixing up. But it's got the best view for sunsets that need to be painted."

She looked pensive. "We still don't know if I'll be able to paint again," she said.

"I told you you'd never be able to play the violin. I never said you'd never be able to paint." It took some painful effort, but he held his arms out to her. "It's a great place for kids," he said quietly.

Jenna choked back a sob as she tried to hug him without hurting him further. She laughed and cried at the same time as Riley cursed at all the wires and IV lines trapping him in the bed.

"I wasn't pushing you away before," he told her as she peppered his face with kisses. "I just wanted to make sure you were safe."

She shook her head. "Don't you know it yet, Riley? As long as I'm with you, I'm always safe."

Epilogue

One year later

Riley knew he was fighting a losing battle with the surf.

Every time he took his board out, he didn't concentrate as he should and fell off. It shouldn't be anything new to him. He'd been doing it since Jenna left the house that morning. She refused to let him go with her, and now he was trying to work off his frustration with the ocean. So far the ocean won.

After a few hours of failure, he was tired, cranky and ready to quit. He walked up the beach with his board tucked under one arm. He stopped when he saw a figure standing above him. With the sun in his eyes, he couldn't see more than a dark blur. He shaded his eyes with his hand and looked up again.

The figure was decidedly feminine wearing a short sundress that displayed a great pair of bare legs. A straw hat was perched on top of her head.

"You used to be pretty good at that," Jenna called out with a mocking lilt. "You must be getting old."

"Old? Hell, I'll show you old," he shot back. She stood there waiting for him as he climbed up the beach. He jammed the end of his surfboard into the sand and turned to face her. "You told me you were going grocery shopping."

She smiled at his gritty accusation. "And I did go grocery shopping."

"And?" He waited, his breath seeming like a solid lump in his chest.

Jenna still smiled. "What would you think of asking Sasha to be our baby's godfather?"

Riley felt an impact that felt roughly like a rocket missile. He was positive he couldn't breathe.

Jenna kept on smiling. There was no doubt her big, bad husband was in a state of shock. She had no doubt that their child would wrap him around its tiny little hand.

At that moment the shock loosened its hold on him and he started to laugh.

"Yes! I'm going to be a father!" he shouted. He grabbed hold of Jenna and danced her in a circle. "Hey, world! I'm going to be a dad!"

He stopped and kept hold of Jenna's shoulders.

"Everything's okay?" he asked, now feeling a tiny niggle of fear. "When?"

She nodded. "Everything is beautiful and in about six and a half months."

Riley kept shaking his head, still unable to believe everything was coming true.

Then he started to laugh.

"There is no way we're telling our kid he or she was conceived the night you persuaded me to pose naked for you," he told her.

She smiled, remembering that afternoon with more than a little fondness.

Riley felt as if he was flying. He picked Jenna up and draped her over his shoulder. He began walking up the beach ignoring her shrieks for him to put her down. He kept on walking until he reached the lanai and entered the house.

The walls were covered with canvases of fairy-tale sunsets and volcanoes showering the earth with red-hot showers of lava. All bore Jenna's initials in the lower left-hand corner.

He kept on walking until they reached their bedroom.

He set her on the bed and followed her down. Jenna gasped as Riley thrust into her. She was more than ready and rose up to meet him, wrapping her legs around his hips to keep him deep inside. When she felt the waves crash over her, she cried out his name and sensed him following her.

They rested awhile, wrapped in each other's arms and Jenna fell into a drowsy sleep. When she awoke and could dredge up enough energy to open her eyes, she glimpsed a flash of rainbow color moving around the room, bouncing off the walls. Her eyes widened when she noticed fluctuating waves of color against the large window.

"Oh, Riley," she breathed his name as she sat up.

She reached out as if she could touch the rainbow sun catcher hanging at the window. "It's beautiful."

He chuckled as he stood over her. He reached for a brown paper bag and held it in front of him.

"You know what you can find at the end of a rainbow?" he asked.

Her lips trembled with laughter. "A pot of gold?"

"Exactly!" He reached into the bag and tossed gold-foil-wrapped chocolate coins across her naked body. "And you," he said, reclining next to her, picking up the coins and allowing them to trickle down between his fingers, "are my end of the rainbow."

Jenna laughed with pure delight as Riley shook his head, sending water droplets everywhere. She reached up and pulled him down. His mouth trailed down her throat.

"And now we both have our pot of gold."

Jenna was again a shivering mass of desire. But deep inside her soul she knew something special had happened between them.

* * * * *

Bestselling author
Joan Elliott Pickart launches
Silhouette's newest cross-line promotion

with
THE
RANCHER
AND
THE
AMNESIAC
BRIDE
Special Edition,
October 1998

Josie Wentworth of the oil-rich Oklahoma Wentworths
knew penthouse apartments and linen finery—not
working ranches...and certainly *not* remote,
recalcitrant ranchers! But one conk to the head and
one slight case of amnesia had this socialite beauty
sharing time and tangling sheets with the cowboy
least likely to pop the question....

And don't miss **The Daddy and the Baby Doctor**
by **Kristin Morgan**, when FOLLOW THAT BABY!
continues in Silhouette Romance in November 1998!

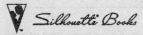

Available at your favorite retail outlet.

Take 2 bestselling love stories FREE

Plus get a FREE surprise gift!

Special Limited-Time Offer

Mail to Silhouette Reader Service™

3010 Walden Avenue
P.O. Box 1867
Buffalo, N.Y. 14240-1867

YES! Please send me 2 free Silhouette Intimate Moments® novels and my free surprise gift. Then send me 6 brand-new novels every month, which I will receive months before they appear in bookstores. Bill me at the low price of $3.57 each plus 25¢ delivery and applicable sales tax, if any.* That's the complete price, and a saving of over 10% off the cover prices—quite a bargain! I understand that accepting the books and gift places me under no obligation ever to buy any books. I can always return a shipment and cancel at any time. Even if I never buy another book from Silhouette, the 2 free books and the surprise gift are mine to keep forever.

245 SEN CH7Y

Name	(PLEASE PRINT)	
Address	Apt. No.	
City	State	Zip

This offer is limited to one order per household and not valid to present Silhouette Intimate Moments® subscribers. *Terms and prices are subject to change without notice. Sales tax applicable in N.Y.

Catch more great

HARLEQUIN™ Movies

featured on

Premiering September 12th
A Change of Place
Starring Rick Springfield and
Stephanie Beacham. Based on the novel
by bestselling author Tracy Sinclair

Don't miss next month's movie!
Premiering October 10th
Loving Evangeline
Based on the novel by *New York Times*
bestselling author Linda Howard

If you are not currently a subscriber to
The Movie Channel, simply call your
local cable or satellite provider for more
details. Call today, and don't miss out
on the romance!

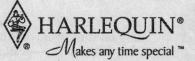

100% pure movies.
100% pure fun.

HARLEQUIN®
Makes any time special ™

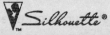

invites you to go West to

Margaret Watson's exhilarating new miniseries.

RODEO MAN...IM #873, August 1998: When ex-rodeo star Grady Farrell set eyes on his childhood sweetheart again, he vowed to put the past behind them. And then he met her—*his*—daughter...and decided to dust off those cowboy boots and stay forever.

FOR THE CHILDREN...IM #886, October 1998: Embittered agent Damien Kane was responsible for protecting beautiful Abby Markham and her twin nieces. But it was Abby who saved him, as she showed him the redeeming power of home and family.

And look for more titles in 1999—
only in Silhouette Intimate Moments!

Available at your favorite retail outlet.

®

Silhouette®

COMING NEXT MONTH